# SPIN CONTROL

# SPIN CONTROL

•

# Holly O'Dell

*AVALON BOOKS*
NEW YORK

Published by Thomas Bouregy & Co., Inc.
160 Madison Avenue, New York, NY 10016

Library of Congress Cataloging-in-Publication Data

O'Dell, Holly.
    Spin Control / Holly O'Dell.
        p. cm.
    ISBN 0-8034-9794-6 (acid-free paper)
    1. Public relations personnel—Fiction. 2. Socialites—New
York (State)—New York—Fiction. 3. New York (N.Y.)—Fiction. 4. Love stories—Fiction. I. Title.

PS3615.D453S65 2006
813'.6—dc22

                                          2006015838

PRINTED IN THE UNITED STATES OF AMERICA
ON ACID-FREE PAPER
BY HADDON CRAFTSMEN, BLOOMSBURG, PENNSYLVANIA

To Kristin, whose patience, wisdom, and advice sustains me, and to Joe, my one and only.

## Chapter One

"Devin Underhill?" I stared at my boss.

"Kate, you're one of my best reps, but I swear that sometimes you live under a rock," Gwen said with a dramatic swipe of her hand, her clunky straight-from-Chinatown bracelets clinking hollowly together. "I know how you frown upon these so-called 'society types,' but you have *got* to know who Devin Underhill is."

Oh, yes, I knew exactly who Devin Underhill was— unabashed New York playboy, heir to the billion-dollar Hotel Bella chain, and the man who just happened to squash my heart like a cockroach two years ago. "It's starting to ring a bell now." I tugged at the neck of my thick pink turtleneck sweater. Probably not the best day to wear it. And was that my throat starting to close up? Oh, great, this was all I needed. I tried to recall proper breathing techniques from the one yoga class I took. Nope, that didn't work.

Gwen turned to face Michael Korten, the publicist transplanted to the New York office from Los Angeles. "Good God, Michael. Please tell me *you* know who he is."

"Of course I do. I emulate his kind." He absent-mindedly smoothed his tie. Sarcasm—or at least I hoped that's what it was—saturated his words.

"As you know—well, maybe not you, Kate, but you can pretend for me—Devin has dated every available, and sometimes not-so-available, socialite in Manhattan. Needless to say, someone of his stature who behaves in such ways gets quite the reputation—and attention from the press."

I squirmed, but tried to cover for it by pretending my black skirt had twisted around. I had been avoiding the New York celebrity-gossip circuit (as much as one can in this town, I suppose) since the breakup with Devin, and, with one comment, Gwen had reminded me of all the voices I had been trying to quell in the past two years. And there I was, behind closed doors with my eccentric boss and a rather stuffy coworker I barely knew, discussing the man who had taken up significant space in my mind.

Michael interrupted my mental wanderings. "So, why does Mr. Underhill need us to do publicity?"

"Two things you should know about this project: Devin's not the one hiring us, and he doesn't know he's our client yet."

I squinted at Gwen, who responded to my confusion. "It's his dad, Fox, who's doing the hiring. Fox's hotels have been experiencing a decline in profits—and image—and he thinks it might be because of his son, or rather his son's reputation. Women and all-night parties seem to be Devin's favorite vices," Gwen said in a confidential tone.

*Great. Thanks, Gwen. Really, could you say one more thing that'll make me want to dive headfirst into the Hudson?*

"And our job is . . . ," Michael watched Gwen quizzically.

"Fox has hired our company to give his son an image makeover."

Gwen leaned in toward Michael and me and shoved her wire-framed glasses back atop her mane of frizzy black hair, a sign that she meant business. "Listen, you two, you're the best reps in this office, so I'm depending on you to make me—I mean us—some money and pull this off. I don't need to tell you that this is the most important project you will ever have at my company, and likely your career."

"Isn't this all kind of a stretch?" Michael frowned as he rubbed one of his eyebrows. "I mean, tying someone's reputation to profits? I may not have an econ degree, but this doesn't add up."

I cringed, because I knew what was coming next. It held the same horrifying yet gleeful fascination for me as watching *The Maury Show* featuring moms awaiting the DNA results of potential fathers. Disaster, waiting to happen. And I couldn't turn away. Michael hadn't been at Burton Relations long enough to know not to criticize the owner of one of the tiniest but most successful publicity firms on the East Coast. I'd seen her fire other reps who had done less to question her judgment. I held my breath and winced.

Gwen shot him her patented withering stare that generally reduced most underlings into contorted heaps. "You're not here to question the reasons. Since when did publicists become the moral authority? Did they teach you that in California, Michael, with your L.A. hotshots?" The rumor buzzing around Michael when he first started at Burton Relations six months ago had been that he was one of the reps responsible for Courtney Love's transformation from bad girl to Hollywood chic. (No word on who was responsible for the transformation undoing all of this.)

Michael didn't seem particularly affected by Gwen's freeze. He just looked at me, looked back at her, and shrugged. "Okay, you've got a point, Gwen. But what kind of challenge, really, are we looking at here?"

I refrained from giving a big "Hmph!" I knew what kind of a challenge we were facing. I could give Michael ten examples from the top of my head; after all, I had experienced at least that many in my six months with Devin. But this was no time for reminiscing or lectures—no question, I had to gracefully remove myself from this project.

I just didn't have a clue as to how to do it.

"It's a huge challenge, Michael, because you're dealing with an outrageous reputation, and that supercedes all else." Gwen used her intimidating-authority-figure voice. "Devin Underhill could rescue baby seals from a clubbing death, but the press would only focus on the wild party that was thrown afterward in honor of his heroic ways."

"Good point, though I will be forever tainted by the baby-seal metaphor." Michael barely smiled—there was that barely-disguised sarcasm again. I glanced at him; he was all business with his carefully pressed white oxford shirt and proper tie. That he helped with the Courtney Love makeover had to be a lie. I had this image of her flailing about his L.A. office while he tried to awkwardly avoid her coming on to him, saying in a stodgy tone, "Ms. Love, we must consider the business at hand." I smirked at the scenario and had almost forgotten why we were all in the office in the first place . . . almost.

"So," Michael continued, "I find it interesting that his dad is hiring a publicity firm." Gwen eyed him, daring him to continue on this line. Instead he put up his hands surrender-style. "I know, I know. Don't question, just do."

I had to give him credit, Michael was quick. He immediately took the cue, his skepticism set aside, if not veiled. "What's our plan of action? Is there a timeline for making this all come together?"

Gwen looked at the ceiling and scratched her neck with her faux fuchsia-colored nails. "I was thinking that you and Kate could hash out the plan. First thing is to gather all the press clippings you can find of our bad boy from the last few years—good, bad, ugly, I don't care. If his name is listed in the *Wall Street Journal*, I want it. If it's on Page Six, I want it." She rose from the perch on her desk and began to pace in front of her windows, in the zone. "The next thing to do is to identify patterns, as we do for all of our clients. I don't care what you do, just make the pieces fit. The problem with this one is that we have to present the information delicately. Remember, Devin has no idea—"

"That we're going to rain on his playboy parade?" Michael suggested dryly.

Gwen didn't miss a beat. "That his dad has this planned for him."

"This should be interesting," Michael observed.

I cleared my throat. "When exactly is he going to break it to Devin?" *And could I be on the other coast by then?*

"When they're in our office tomorrow."

"What?" Michael and I cried in unison.

"Settle down, settle down," Gwen assured us, her skittish minions. "I told you at the beginning of this conversation, you two can handle it. If it means you stay up all night, then take a three-day weekend on me."

Michael was incredulous. "You mean that we have to have our proposal done in twenty-four hours? What about our other clients?"

"I'm going to put some junior account executives on them," she said carelessly. "Might as well throw them a bone. Listen, I can tell you that Fox Underhill is paying us very good money to do this for him and his son. And that information doesn't leave this room." Gwen loved using that line. Often I would get this image of Gwen's office bulging with information that wasn't allowed to leave her office. Would the tidbits eventually explode out the door and rain down on the desks of unsuspecting executives?

I was staring out the window watching traffic pass when Gwen took notice of my lack of enthusiasm. "Kate, you haven't said much, and frankly, dear, you're being an airhead." I knew how much Gwen adored labeling her workers, and if this one incident would forever brand me as a ditz, I had to take control of my emotions—as if that were realistic at the moment. But just then, Gwen softened a bit. "Is everything okay?"

I tried to muster my buried courage. "Um, actually, I would like to talk to you after this meeting." Michael quickly turned his head toward me, and I flushed. "It's nothing, really. Just a few ideas I'd like to run past you, Gwen."

"Let's have Michael stay and hear them."

"It's about a different project I'm working on." Another lie.

Gwen smirked. "Sure, whatever you say. Before we let Michael go, we should get a plan together today. You can have Rita pull press clippings and do online searches. Then you two should put your heads together and come up with a tactful but persuasive way to present your findings to Devin and his dad." She returned to the desk and folded her hands prayer-style. "Please, please, *please* remember that Devin doesn't even know what's happening. I talked to Fox earlier today, and his plan is to invent some meeting for him and Devin to attend in the building, and oops, he's just gonna pop in and see how his old friend Gwen Burton is doing. Before you know it, we'll *all* be chatting like old friends—one of whom needs a new public personality, mind you. They'll be here at ten o'clock tomorrow, so at eight, I want to look over what you came up with and offer suggestions." She looked back and forth between the two of us. "Got it?"

"Of course!" Michael replied a little too eagerly. I think he and I both knew that something this dicey, this much of a stretch, was never so smooth. And to get it done in record time only added to my stress.

Michael rose from his chair; he had abnormally straight posture. "I'm going to get started. I'll let you two have your talk. Oh, Kate, do you want to meet over lunch?"

"Can we do it after? I have lunch plans." Not really, but I was about to. I needed to meet with my best friend, Anna, so she could help me process (translation: overanalyze) the sticky problem I had just acquired. Besides, after the conversation I planned on having with Gwen, I'd be off the project and would have no need to talk about Devin ever again.

"I guess I'll just catch you this afternoon." Michael quietly closed Gwen's door.

For about thirty seconds, the only thing audible was my accelerating heartbeat. In that time, I devised ways to tell Gwen about my past with Devin. Surely Gwen would see the ethical conflicts with me working as my ex's right-hand woman. Alternatively, she could fire me for not being up-front right away. No, she couldn't do that, could she?

I had been on a four-year roller-coaster ride at Burton Relations, and this is what I wanted—the assignment that was going to push me to the top of that last hill, with no fear of ever dropping again. It just was too bad that an ex-boyfriend was going to be the vehicle to get me there.

"Looks like I'll be the first one to talk." Gwen finally broke the silence with a stern look that could stop traffic.

My relationship with Gwen was a complex one—at one moment I could be teasing her, and fearing her the next. But no matter how I felt, I have always respected Gwen for starting her own PR firm on her thirtieth birthday twenty-some years ago. In my time with Gwen, I had seen turnover-much of which came from those used to working in conventional agencies who couldn't understand why this outlandish woman would actually make her representatives do their own research or attend the events they promoted on weekends. Somehow I had broken from that pack. Gwen always said that she saw a part of herself in me, which scared me because I never knew which part.

"I think I know why you're being shifty," Gwen smugly remarked. "I know why you're so reluctant to work on the project."

How did Gwen know? And why did she put me on this project knowing what she knew? Perhaps it was a test—one at which I was failing miserably. That still didn't answer the how. Fox Underhill had only met me once while Devin and I dated, so he certainly wouldn't remember me and certainly couldn't know that I worked at this firm. I wasn't even sure if Devin remembered what I did for a living, so that couldn't be it. "Am I that easy to read?" I asked sheepishly.

"You're worried about working with Michael, aren't you?"

As if. I let out a screech. "God, no. Michael is great! I mean, I barely know him, but he seems really smart and good at what he does. My problem is much deeper than that." Gwen crossed her arms, her lime-green blouse bunching up. She pulled the glasses from the top of her head and peered at me with curious eyes.

I opened my mouth but was greeted with silence. I couldn't tell Gwen. I had the strange sense that she would be disappointed in me. "It's just that I'm not cut out for this celebrity stuff. You know that. I like to work on products and properties, not figureheads." At least I had moved from telling lies to telling half-truths.

Gwen stood up and sat on the edge of her desk, about two inches from my face. "I have a reason for doing this," she said in a conspiratorial whisper. "The thought of retirement is always crossing my mind. Of course, could I trust someone to carry on the Burton name? It certainly won't be children—it's a little too late for that—too bad my cats couldn't run this place! Wait, where was I? Oh, yes." She walked over to the door to check that it was closed completely. "It's no secret, Kate, that you're one of my favorites at this place." She closed her overmascaraed eyes and inhaled deeply through her nose. "If you nail this project, you will be a partner in this firm. And at twenty-nine, you'd be the youngest ever, I might add. Even younger than I was when I started the business, my dear."

My heart resumed its incessant pounding. This was it. This was the crucial step I needed to make. It's what I had been working toward since I'd moved to New York six years earlier after a short-lived tenure in hell covering weekly city council meetings for a small, sub-urban newspaper on the outskirts of Kansas City. Un-fortunately, after the move it took me two years of additional hell, Manhattan-style, to find Gwen, but I found her. And I had jockeyed for position with the oth-ers my age, working my way up the food chain, slaver-ing over the idea of running a business of my own some day.

Now Gwen was offering me what could be the most professionally and financially lucrative proposal I had ever gotten. If only I could get the position by market-ing Gucci handbags!

I took the bait, perhaps a little too quickly. Certainly no self-respecting career goddess would let a chintzy ex-boyfriend push her off the path to success, would she? *This is what I want,* I repeated.

So why was a nagging feeling tugging deep within me?

I couldn't rely on my gut instincts anymore, as they often were just veiled paranoia. For now, I had to be a researcher, observing her subjects objectively. The self-affirmation litany began: *I am a skilled public rela-tions representative assigned to the most crucial project of my career. I am a skilled public relations representa-tive who, so help me Higher Power, is going to have to come face to face tomorrow with the man who—*

Okay, maybe self-affirmations were overrated. Just faking it sounded good.

I eyed Gwen eyeing me, curiosity overtaking her face. I gave Gwen what surely was my most winsome smile. "Thanks for the offer. You're right, I should be able to handle a job like this." I should. I would. And I saw it in my mind's eye, the perfect execution, and myself several months later, sitting in this chair ready to sign the appropriate paperwork indicating that I was a partner.

"There's my girl!" Gwen almost leapt. "I was worried there for a while."

I rose and walked toward the door. "No need to worry. I'm going to catch up with Michael."

"By the way, Kate." I pivoted to face Gwen. "Devin Underhill is only a New York celebrity—not internationally known, but suitable to be auctioned off as an eligible bachelor at a fundraiser in SoHo." Gwen paused. "What I'm trying to say is that you shouldn't be intimidated by his quasi-celebrity status."

I gave a halfhearted nod. If only Gwen knew that his place on the social ladder was the least of my concerns with Devin.

## Chapter Two

"I feel like I'm in junior high," I said, hypnotically pushing around the red-curry chicken on my plate. "It's been two years, and we only dated for six months, yet one mention of his name and *pfft,* I unravel faster than a predictable plot. I almost feel like a fraud. I claim to be this strong, independent, urban woman, but listening to myself makes me want to gag."

Anna vehemently shook her head, her long, loose, enviable red curls bouncing vibrantly. "You *are* strong, independent, and urban. You're also human. Welcome to the masses."

In work, I knew I could command a room full of executives. In love, however, I crumpled when a man dumped me. "So why can't I transform myself?"

"Quit acting like there's something wrong with you! Men break our hearts." She folded her arms across her tiny black T-shirt, which simply stated *Nerds Rule.*

13

"We cry and watch soppy movies and eat Ben & Jerry's until we can't see. That's life. Sometimes it takes longer than we like to admit. Granted two years is a little long, but hey, who am I to judge? We both know how I am in the relationship world."

"Speaking of relationship worlds, how's Tommy? I haven't heard you talk about him in a few weeks." Her guilty look was a dead giveaway. "Uh-oh. Is it time for another soul-cleansing trip?"

When it came to dating, Anna was the opposite of me—and most women our age, apparently. She enjoyed the breakup more than the hookup. Whenever she ended a relationship (and she was always the one who ended it), she took a vacation to "cleanse the soul." Then she got right back into the scene, anxiously awaiting her next trip—um, relationship.

Anna tried for penitent but quickly slipped into mischief, green eyes flashing. "I can't help it! We're just too similar, and *blech,* who wants that? So I think we're going to have a little talk tonight."

I rolled my eyes. "If only it were that simple for me. You know, it's not like I've been pining for Devin or anything . . . I've simply blocked him out."

"That's exactly your problem." Anna pointed her fork at me for emphasis. "You never processed any of this stuff so he's taken on this godlike thing for you. And now here you sit, totally stressed over seeing him after two years. Sooner or later, you've got to deal with it, sweetie."

"I know," I muttered.

"You realize that you were basically offered a partnership in the firm today, right? I can't help but wonder if you're trying to sabotage yourself."

"I see that your bachelor's in psychology really does come in handy once in a while." Anna and I both graduated from the University of Missouri. Fortunately, Anna had disliked her temp job as an envelope stuffer post-graduation as much as I'd abhorred my job in birdcage-liner hell, and after only one week of scheming, we agreed to move immediately to New York City in pursuit of the glamorous dream we had seen in dozens of movies. Silly us.

Anna had worked odd jobs all over Manhattan for the past six years but finally found her niche as a makeup artist for off-Broadway plays. Although she enjoyed analyzing all the has-beens and wannabes of the New York theater scene, she saved her best psychoanalysis for me.

"I wouldn't label this as psychology. It's tough love."

"Tough love? Well, you're really gonna pull out the tough love now, because I have a confession." I paused. "I sometimes still listen to the sad rejected-girl CD I made."

*"Girl, Dumped"?* Anna shook her head. "I should have tossed that CD onto the subway tracks when I had the chance. I mean, 'Always on My Mind' by Willie Nelson? 'Even Now' by Barry Manilow? 'Sad Songs Say So Much' by Elton John? Good god, girl. I said it then, and I'll say it now. If you're going to grieve, at least pick something a little more modern."

It was this tough love that Anna often had to implement the first few months after the breakup. Now she leaned across the table, pushing away her plate of half-eaten pineapple fried rice. "You know what, Kate? You're a lot stronger than you give yourself credit for. What did you lose, 10 pounds after you broke up with that bastard? Got a promotion? You taught community ed classes, for god's sake. You had the chance to explore who you are and not let some guy's rejection dictate that."

"Sure, and let's count all the dates I've had since then."

"What do you mean? I've tried to set you up."

"Yeah, with either your gay actor friends or their freaky directors."

Perplexed, Anna looked up at the ceiling. Even she couldn't remember the last date I had. "Oh, wait! What about that blind date you had? The scientist guy?"

Oh yeah, the blind date. The blind date who just happened to make reservations at Balthazar, the restaurant where Devin and I went for our first date.

This was my life. Thousands of restaurants in this darn city, and this was the one Mr. Blind Date picked. It was destined to be a tragicomedy, and a miserably boring one, at that. He might have been a chemist, but the chemistry between us was pathetic. He droned on about his latest project at the lab and I gave myself credit for managing a polite nod, just like a good Midwestern girl is taught to do. The worst part was I couldn't help but scan the restaurant for Devin.

And he was there.

Okay, not him, but his cologne, which I inhaled when a patron wearing Devin's signature scent passed by the table. Instantly, my eyes went into leak mode. When the tears started splashing on my braised lamb, I knew I had to do something. Without explanation, I fled to the bathroom. Fifteen or twenty minutes later, after the worst of the tears was over and the puffiness had diminished enough to accept as passable, I returned to the table.

Only to find a credit-card receipt and a note that read, "Sorry I left but I cant date some one who has undelt with issues."

How perfect—getting a kiss-off note from an illiterate. It was meant to be, then, because I couldn't date someone who couldn't spell or hyphenate properly.

I shook my head, attempting to rid it of the debilitating tale. "Dating just isn't something I do very well. I think you need to be genetically programmed or something. And Devin *definitely* isn't in the cards. So what do I do?"

Anna tucked a renegade curl behind her ear. "Kate, listen to me. Being on this project is the best thing that could happen to you. It'll be liberating. You haven't seen him in two years." She laughed. "He is going to be putty in your hands. His dad is hiring you to publicly babysit him. It's humiliating! You're in control here. Frankly, you've always been in control. Maybe now is the time to start admitting it."

"How do you always know what to say?"

Anna shrugged. "It's what keeps me mysterious."

I smiled and checked my watch. "Well, I have quite the afternoon and evening ahead of me. Michael and I are getting together tonight to come up with something to present to Devin and his dad."

Anna's eyes widened. "Michael? Cute California Michael?"

I snorted. She had seen him briefly a few months ago when she paid me an office visit; only she could think of Mr. Stiff as cute. "More like Socially Awkward California Michael. Yeah, he stopped me on my way out the door to meet you and reminded me that the only way we'll meet our deadline is by working tonight. And since I don't want to die of boredom at his house, I told him to stop by my place."

"Oh, come on. Aren't you just a little attracted to him? That sunkissed brown hair?"

"Highlights," I offered.

"And he has those gorgeous hazel eyes."

"Contacts, I'm sure."

"And that nice, straight jawline."

"Plastic surgery, probably."

Anna pointed at me. "Admit it! You noticed."

"*Doy,* I'm not blind. He's just not my type, and besides, he's kind of stilted anyway."

Anna looked at me speculatively. "Girl, this could be the antidote you've been waiting for."

"Look at me. I am in no shape to enjoy his company while I figure out how to remake the image of an ex-boyfriend. And like I just said, he's a little uptight for my taste."

"Then you have another project on your hands—loosen that boy up!" Anna winked.

My eyes frantically scanned the Thai restaurant. I hushed Anna, but that didn't stop the dicey commentary.

"What, you worried that someone you've never met might have heard me? Maybe a little lovin' is what you and Michael both need," she chortled.

I slid down my chair, though that certainly didn't hide my burning face.

"You're just as uptight as he is! In all seriousness, Kate, there are a lot of women throughout the country who would die to give their exes a personality makeover."

I raised my eyebrows. "Lucky me."

## Chapter Three

The last thing I wanted to do was pore over press clippings from the last five years that illustrated Devin's womanizing ways. Interestingly, there was a gap in 2004 when we dated. Devin had shielded me from the spotlight. He had said he was protecting me from the media glare, but a pessimistic voice deep within my subconscious told me that he didn't want us to be seen together. Whenever I brought it up with him, he'd dismiss me. "Quit being ridiculous," he would whisper in my ear. "Besides, you're too sweet to be under gossip-hound scrutiny."

One picture of us had found its way into *New York* magazine, however, and I kept the clipping folded up in my dictionary on the page with the word *mystery*. I had attended a multiple sclerosis benefit with Devin. Under the picture read the caption, "Devin Underhill, vice

20

president of Hotel Bella, Inc., with an unidentified guest."

Unidentified guest. That pretty much summed up our whole relationship. The picture had appeared in the magazine two months after our breakup. Needless to say, I spent another two months scrutinizing the photo daily.

The only saving grace was that it was actually a presentable picture—good thing, too, or else I would have had to move to Saskatchewan. My wavy chestnut hair barely touched my shoulders, which I'd shown off in a black halter top gown. When Anna first saw the picture, she immediately called me at work. "What a babe you are. You look better than any starlet he could have brought to one of these gala events. Who did your makeup?" Anna, of course, had done my makeup for my first—and last—major outing with Devin. She had pulled out the photo shoot lights and everything. Rather intimidating, really, trying not to sweat off the layers of caked-on goo. "I mean, I knew I did a good job on you, but you surpassed my wildest dreams." I'll admit, I'd known she was overcompensating since at that point the breakup was still fairly fresh, but I took what I could get.

I looked at the photo now, shifting my attention to Devin. Hot, there was no two ways about it. His jet-black hair provided the perfect contrast to his crystal-blue eyes. They gave me flutters every time I saw him. And at six feet five, he'd made me feel petite—something my five-foot, nine-inch frame never allowed around most men. And those broad shoulders. Yum.

I cut off that line of thought with a sigh. Where was the justice? Blessed with a fortune, blessed with perfect genes . . . I looked at the photo one last time. Maybe I wasn't Devin's typical girlfriend, but at that moment, in that picture, I had believed that we were the perfect fit.

I dropped the picture when my door buzzer sounded. Michael had arrived for our evening appointment. Tripping over the Devin-related magazines and Internet printouts scattered on the floor, I sauntered toward the door. I flipped the deadbolt, turned the handle, and found a box brimming with magazines practically in my lap.

"Sorry," Michael said, clutching at it. "I was just leaning it against the door jamb."

"Whoa, you're certainly ahead of me on the research," I commented.

"Do you know how many magazines Gwen has in the storage room? Everything that's been in print on the East Coast since 1972, I swear. I grabbed everything I could from '95 through now." Michael grunted as he threw the box on the floor next to my research materials. He was still wearing his work clothes.

It was awkward having a man in my house after all these years, even if he was just a platonic coworker. Before Michael arrived, I hid all personal items—even the innocuous stuff, like my toothbrush.

I watched him scan my loft—the hardwood flooring, the shadows of the walls, and angles of the ceiling. It might not have been ultra-modern like the condo he likely lived in, but he seemed genuinely impressed.

That is, until he opened his mouth.

"Wow! What's Gwen paying you to live in a loft like this?"

Not only stodgy, but tacky. I bristled. "Probably not as much as you, considering that she talked about you every day for the two weeks before you started at the office. She loved the fact that she was getting one of the hottest publicists from L.A."

"One of the hottest publicists, huh? That's flattering. She speaks highly of you, too."

"Well, I work hard," I said with a nonchalant shrug. "I do pretty well, but I choose to have a great place rather than great furniture." Michael and I simultaneously looked at the two main pieces in my living room—a red-and-gold loveseat I'd found at an estate sale on a road trip to the Pennsylvania countryside, and a used purple-velvet couch an old neighbor abandoned in her apartment. "Some day I hope to have the trendy New Yorker lifestyle, but for now, this is home."

"Trendy New Yorker? I think you're well on your way." *Could that be flirting?* I wondered, but immediately reneged that thought. He wouldn't know what flirting was if a woman brazenly threw herself at him.

"Can I get you something to drink?" I said, trying to disrupt the disturbing mental image I had just created. "I have water and soda. Pretty basic."

"I'll have some water thanks." Michael followed me into the kitchen and leaned against the counter. "So, do you find it odd that Gwen seems really wrapped up in this Underhill account? I don't want to sound arrogant, but I've had much more challenging subjects. I mean, he's a dim playboy."

I thrust the bottle of water at Michael. No need to be reminded of my poor choice in dating Devin. I shifted to my business persona. "I did some more research on Hotel Bella itself, and yes, it is losing profits. And in recent surveys, guests have indicated their displeasure with the franchise's image. But how "Father Fox" connected this demise to Devin is beyond me."

"The best guess I have is that Hotel Bella has positioned itself with high-end, posh accommodations offered by a well-to-do but still down-to-earth family," Michael said dryly. "And now that you have the heir to this regarded business running rampant all over the city, people are starting to get turned off. Or at least that is what we say tomorrow. It's impossible to connect something as objective as statistics to something as subjective as behavior."

I suppressed a big, fat eye-roll at his stuffy language. "Did you get that out of a brochure?"

Michael cleared his throat. "Okay, let me refocus: Why does Gwen care so much?"

Michael was right. Gwen did seem overzealous about the whole thing. "For starters, she wasn't shy about how much dough she's gonna bring in from the Underhills. But I can't help but wonder if she might not have a crush on Fox. Here he is, a good-looking, widowed, wealthy man whom she referred to as an 'old friend' earlier today. All I know is that I don't care what the reason is because—" I stopped myself. Gwen had promised me a partnership, but I couldn't assume she had done the same for Michael. But apparently she had.

"Oh, you mean becoming a partner? Yeah, she told

me that she offered it to you and asked if I'd be interested in joining the club."

I felt slighted. Why would Gwen want that yawner to run her company? Was she just doing a little double-talk trick with us? Why would a publicist use that trick against her own? But now was not the time to jump to conclusions. Surely Gwen wouldn't manipulate me like that. And the last thing I wanted was for Michael to think I was obsessing over the situation.

"Well, if we do become partners," I grinned, "the first order of business is to take down that 'Hang in There, Baby' poster. You know, the one with the cat dangling from the scratching post?"

Michael laughed. "Yeah, I think she stole that one from my third-grade classroom."

I put my hand up. "Wait. Where's my computer? I've got to write a press release."

"Huh?"

"I think that's the first time I've ever heard you laugh. This is news."

"I laugh," he objected.

"I don't think so."

"Of course I do."

"Nope."

"That's because you don't joke in New York. Everybody's always so busy being aloof and urban and ironic. Everybody thinks they're in a Woody Allen movie."

"So, if Woody Allen is our director, who's the director for the L.A. crowd?"

His eyes crinkled with humor. "Ah, everybody's the

director of their own movie there." Huh, Anna was pretty observant the first time she met him. His eyes were hazel, and I had noticed for the first time the little dark flecks near the middle.

I swallowed. "We really should get started on this." Yes, and get out of the kitchen into the nice, open living room. "How about you start going through all those magazines while I whip up some strong coffee for myself?"

I returned to the kitchen and dug for my espresso maker. "Hey," Michael yelled from the living room. "Is this a first edition of *Catcher in the Rye*?"

I peeked my head around the corner. "Yup. I got it as a gift from my mom. I was obsessed with that book in high school. Could really relate to that teen-angst thing."

He carefully flipped through the delicate pages. "Hmm, and I thought only guys could relate to Holden Caufield." We shared a look, one of those that's a beat longer than it should be. I turned back to my cupboards, plowing through the plates and bowls obstructing my way to my coffee maker.

"Wow, your hair's really long in this picture," Michael said from the doorway.

I jumped and knocked my head on the cabinet. When I came out and saw him holding the photo from *New York* magazine, all I wanted to do was crawl back in. How had he gone from J.D. Salinger to Kate Brown history in one minute?

Michael stared at the photo, looking horribly confused, or maybe lost. I tried to explain. "Yeah, I got it cut right after that picture was taken and my friend Anna said I looked like Halle Berry but I really thought I looked more like the love child of Rod Stewart and Elton John after he got his weave, so I cried for two days. Anyway, you probably don't care since guys usually don't give a crap about bad haircuts but I am glad that it's grown out a bit and I think this length is still considered short but not as short as it was that fateful day when no one stopped me from getting my hair chopped." I stopped.

Michael grinned slightly as he watched my cheeks redden. "Okay, do you want to breathe and tell me the real story?"

"It was two years ago, we only went out for six months, and please don't tell Gwen because she'll fire me for withholding this information from her."

"So you dated Devin Underhill," he said thoughtfully. "Hunh."

"What's with the 'hunh'?" I bridled.

"He just doesn't seem to be your type."

My type? What did Michael know about my type? Of course, it could just have been guy-speak for "You don't seem like *his* type." Instead, I gave Michael the answer I thought he was looking for. "Everybody's got a past, and that's mine," I said. So it was a movie line, but I wasn't above using whatever tools came to hand. Besides, it was New York and ironic. "Look, I was younger and didn't have my priorities straight. Now I do, and can we please just forget about it?" My voice was headed dangerously close to squeaky. "I assure you, Michael, it's in the past and it's not going to interfere with this project. I am all about professionalism, and I ask the same of you."

"How did it end?"

Oh, that was the capper. He wanted me to trot out my romantic failures for him? Not in this lifetime. "It's not important," I said coolly. "Trust me. I want nothing more to do with him, romantically, anyway. Unfortunately, he has become my ticket to succeeding at Gwen's firm, or so she alleges, and I am doing my best to forget that we ever dated."

"How did it end?" he repeated, idly curious.

"How do you think it ended?" I snapped, wondering why I was on the hot seat in my own home. "He lost interest. We were just a mismatch from the start. You know, forcing something to be there that shouldn't have gone past the second date?" I quickly turned to my espresso maker, never more interested in making some high-caf brew as I was at that moment.

Michael followed me to the kitchen. "So, do you think—"

"I don't want to be rude, but I really don't want to discuss it anymore. Can we just go back to the living room and start our pitch for tomorrow morning?"

Michael ran a hand through his brown hair, which surprised me because I didn't think he'd want to mess it up. "So you were working at Burton Relations when you were seeing Devin, right? Isn't he going to suspect something when Daddy brings him to our office?"

I briefly panicked; Gwen would have me on a one-way train to Philly by sundown tomorrow. But then I remembered who we were talking about.

"Trust me, he won't remember where I work. Heck, I'll be surprised if he even remembers my name." That's exactly what I needed, a reminder of Devin's selfishness to keep me motivated to stay on the account.

With a sense of empowerment, I breezed past Michael, sat down on the floor of my den, and plowed through the magazines with the efficiency of a factory worker. Michael followed my lead.

The articles definitely came under the heading of too much information, featuring the gaudy details of his recent romantic encounters.

"Gotta hand it to the guy, he gets around," Michael said mildly.

"Would I sound naïve if I said that he wasn't like this when we were dating?" I shook my head in bewilderment. "So he liked to look at the ladies, but that was about it. He enjoyed his drinks, sure, but he was never sloppy around me, at least."

Michael was concentrating on his laptop and didn't reply.

I exhaled a relieved sigh when I knew that Michael wasn't paying attention. This was the Michael I knew, not the guy who kept asking me what happened with Devin, and looking like he actually cared. I grabbed another magazine and halfheartedly flipped through it. Okay, maybe I was flipping through my memories more than the magazine in front of me, but it was all data.

As though he'd heard my thought, Michael raised his

head. "I don't suppose you know anything from your time with Devin that will help us, do you? I mean, we have to think of a way to straighten him out."

I thought of the end of our relationship, dates cancelled not by Devin but by his assistant, proclamations that he would be settling if he stayed with me, and, of course, Devin's infamous ways of "shielding" me from the public. It was all too humiliating to share with anyone but Anna—and certainly not Michael. I feared mockery. "Let me think about it," I evaded.

"Ugh." Michael sounded genuinely disgusted.

"What?"

"It's nothing."

"It doesn't sound like nothing." He attempted to tuck the magazine away, but I hastily reached over and snatched it out of his hand.

There Devin was, eyes half open, with his hand cupping a buttock of the April Playmate. I slid the magazine back to Michael.

"There's being a playboy, and then there's hanging lecherously all over a Playmate." Michael shook his head. "Creep."

For the next two hours, we urgently took notes on paper and on our laptops, attempting to put all our information together for a cohesive presentation. We agreed not to make this a personal attack on Devin, which went completely against my instinct.

"So, earlier today, you seemed pretty confident that this was going to be a cakewalk. But I'm still curious to know who you worked with in L.A." Please say Courtney Love. Please say Courtney Love.

"Ah, just the usuals. Derrik Train is a big one."

"Yeah, I don't much get into that whole scene, but he does sound somewhat familiar."

"Derrik plays the main character on *Long Beach*— you know, a *Dallas* for the Gen-Xers? Anyway, he took a joyride with a young woman who claimed to be a reporter for a college newspaper. He was driving pretty fast, missed a curve, and wrapped the girl and the Mercedes around a telephone pole."

I gasped. "That's awful! What happened to the girl?" And how did I miss this whole story when it happened? That's why it's better to market products rather than celebrities, I suppose. Or that may be what made Michael such a great publicist—he made us all forget that it ever occurred.

"Well, the good news is that they both walked away without a scratch. The bad news was that the girl lied about her age—she was a 14-year-old fan."

"And, of course, you had to swoop in and try to spin Derrik's bad judgment?"

"Yeah, my boss really wanted me to play up that this young teenage girl was a floozy and all but seduced Derrik, but I just couldn't do that. I mean, she's just a kid. Derrik should've known better."

"Wow, that's dicey," I said, shaking my head. "What did you do?"

Michael shrugged. "I got on the phone with the tabloids to tell them that it was one big misunderstanding. Derrik assumed she was older, he made a mistake, nothing happened, Derrik was a perfect gentleman, police reports show there was no alcohol or drugs in his system, it was a dark road with a curve, he was actually bringing the girl back home when he realized the mix-up with the girl's age . . ." Michael sighed through his nose. "See why I needed to get out of L.A.?"

I cleared my throat. "Well, should we get back to Devin? As far as I know, he hasn't done anything like Derrik, but it sounds like we'll still be able to strong-arm him tomorrow."

"Strong-arm him? Isn't that a wrestling move?" Michael said wryly.

"Hey, I was raised in the Midwest. It's what I know."

"Guess I'm not surprised." He spoke with a hint of condescension.

I opened my mouth to reply, but quickly shut it. What did that mean, 'Guess I'm not surprised'?

"Why so quiet?" he asked a little while later.

Yes, go ahead and insult me, and then wonder why I'm not chatty. "I'm contemplating whether I should use The Claw or The Hulk Hogan on you, that's all."

He set aside his laptop, clutching his gut from laughter. "You didn't think I was serious about the wrestling comment, did you?"

"For starters, it's 'rasslin,' not 'wrestling.' " I sheepishly joked back. "Sorry for getting a little saucy back there. I just get a lot of 'you know you're from Missouri if' commentary out here, so I *might* be a little quick with the sword."

*"Might?"* Michael winked.

I felt myself blush. I prayed he didn't see that.

## Chapter Four

I flipped the switch inside my office door, and the fluorescent lights hummed a moment and then blinked on. There was no natural light coming in through my window at this time of day, in this dreary March. The pitiless clock on the wall boasted 6:45.

This was supposed to be my morning of victory, or so Anna had told me. I was supposed to bound in to the meeting bursting with health and style. Instead, I was creeping into the office before the paperboys had even finished their deliveries, my eyes still stinging from the sleep I didn't get. Not that I hadn't tried after I'd sent Michael home at about 2 A.M. I'd tossed. I'd turned.

I'd given up.

On top of the sleepless misery, I couldn't bear the thought of watching cheesy early-morning television. The only alternatives were staring absently at my closet, waiting for a knock-Devin-dead outfit to throw

33

itself at me, or coming to work two hours before every-one else in Manhattan. I chose both, only the latter of which was successful. After pulling shirts from dresser drawers and skirts from hangers for an hour, I begrudg-ingly decided on a sleeveless black cowl-neck sweater, a brick-red skirt that hit just above the knee, and strappy, wedged Mary Janes.

I sauntered to the office kitchen and grabbed a bottle of water. What I really needed was an I.V. of java, but getting within ten feet of coffee would guarantee that it would become an unwelcome addition to my already shaky outfit. Instead, I opted for a nice, cold bottle of water—safe option.

Back at my desk, I stared at my notes, waiting for in-spiration to hit. I supposed that I didn't need to worry about it; after all, the plan Michael and I had set into place was pretty straight-forward: Don't threaten Devin, be his friend, give him a list of high-end events to attend and people to be around, and so on.

I didn't much care for the idea of poring through all these notes again, but still, my experience as a public relations executive told me that preparation was essen-tial. Anna always said I was blessed with the gift of speaking off the cuff, but overconfidence in such an ability could devour me. I imagined worst-case scenar-ios of blanking when Fox Underhill asked me about the strategy for Devin or when Devin himself questioned my involvement in the project. Shaking my head to clear it of the negative visions, I grabbed my notes, cir-cled my office, and began practicing how I would start the meeting before handing it off to Michael.

"Well, well, well, this must be the famed Devin Underhill I've been hearing so much about." I extended my hand for an imaginary handshake. "It's a pleasure to place the man with the name—all those pictures in the magazines really don't do you justice." I smacked an open palm against my forehead, partly out of frustration, partly out of embarrassment for myself.

"Devin is never going to go for this." I said as I turned back to the desk to scavenge my notes. "He will blow my cover, we will lose the account, Gwen will fire me, and I will be shuffling through the streets of New York in a tattered overcoat, pushing a shopping cart and talking to myself like the crazy person I am."

"You should charge admission for that routine."

I gasped and jumped back at the voice. There, leaning against the doorframe, was Michael, dressed in a navy-blue jacket and a white Oxford shirt with one button undone.

"No tie."

"Good morning to you too." Michael looked down. "Oh, should I have worn one?"

"No, I'm just going into shock because I've never seen you without a tie, that's all."

"I see that your wit is always on, twenty-four-seven."

"What can I say? All that sleep I got last night just jazzed me up." I picked up my folder with notes and immediately dropped it on my desk. "Just so you know, when this meeting is done, I'm leaving for a big, fattening, fancy lunch and I'm not coming back until tomorrow morning."

"That sounds pretty desperate."

"The situation is pretty desperate."

"I don't think so." He stepped closer to me. "I think we've got a plan and a good approach. I think we'll do fine. Either way, I'm tagging along with you to your big, fattening, fancy lunch."

I gave a humorless laugh. "Trust me, as soon as Devin figures out what we're talking about, he's going to be ticked off and gone, pretty much in that order."

"I'm not so sure. I think he'll stay, if only to try to make himself look good."

"Wait, wasn't I the one who dated him?"

"True, but I'm betting he's going to stay."

"You serious about that?"

He blinked. "Why? What do you have in mind?"

"I think Devin is going to storm out of the meeting and I'm willing to make a bet on it. If he stays, I have to buy your meal. If he goes, you are picking up my *entire* bill. Overpriced hors d'oeuvres and all." I grinned confidently because there was no doubt in my mind how this meeting would end. Whenever Devin didn't get his way or didn't know how to handle an adverse situation, he left the room. Toward the end of our relationship, Devin and I had been discussing what movie to see. Devin wanted an action flick; I wanted a comedy. When I pointed out to him that the last three movies we had watched had been action-oriented, Devin turned his back on me, walked out of my apartment, and didn't talk to me for three days.

"It's a deal," Michael said as he shook my hand firmly. A soft hand, yet still masculine.

I broke from the handshake and smoothed my skirt.

"Now if you'll excuse me, Michael, I have some notes that I must blankly stare at." As I sat down at my desk, I watched Michael leave my office. I could not wait to win our bet so I could show him what girls from the Midwest really do for grins: eat till we can't see—and watch the boys pick up the tab. I giggled girlishly. This was going to be fun. Michael? Fun? What an interesting concept.

"It's showtime." Gwen peered into my office as I applied powder to my face. "This isn't a beauty contest, Brown. Devin and Fox are going to be here in five minutes, so pack up your girlie stuff and get in the main conference room."

When I first started at Gwen's firm, I teared up each time she barked orders like this one. But over the years, I learned that Gwen's drill-sergeant demeanor was how she channeled her stress. With that, I looked up from my compact and saluted—okay, more like shielded myself from her blinding yellow suit and matching pumps. Gwen shook her head and walked toward the meeting room.

An eerie, rather unnatural calm had set over me about twenty minutes earlier. I gathered my materials and walked briskly toward the conference room. There sat Michael, Gwen, and Fox, but no Devin. I set my handful of papers and folders on the cherry-wood table and walked toward Fox. Gwen stood up to introduce us. "Fox, this is Kate Brown. Kate, Fox Underhill."

I was reminded how Devin got his striking features. Fox was about six-foot-three with silver hair contrasting tanned skin, presumably from all his travels. His blue eyes were a shade darker than his son's; they offered a sense of genuineness, but you could tell they meant business.

I'd had a similar reaction to Fox the last—and only—time I met him. Devin needed to stop at his father's downtown penthouse, and I had to practically beg to come in with him. When I entered the apartment, I maintained my awe as best I could. It was more impressive than Devin's Park Avenue abode, and I thought that was a jaw-dropper. But there in Fox's home, I was experiencing a completely different lifestyle.

The living room alone, which was the only part of Fox's home I saw, looked like a museum. The floors, Devin later told me, were made of wood imported from Africa. An eighteenth-century French writing table with bronze legs stood in the foyer, while intricate Turkish rugs blanketed the hardwood floors. Two mottled European vases with rich greens and blues on mahogany stands were placed on either side of Fox's sleek, mocha-colored couch. Off to the side I caught a glimpse of the den, which held an antique baby-grand piano—another relic in this untouchable dwelling.

I walked toward the big picture windows, where a stunning view of Manhattan's finest buildings glowed in the setting autumn sun. Devin picked up his items from his father's place and pulled me away from the majestic scene. As we exited, Fox walked in wearing his tennis whites—so apropos for this situation, I thought smugly.

"Hi, Dad," Devin said abruptly as he grabbed my hand and pulled me to the door.

"Devin, aren't you going to introduce me to your

friend?" Fox had a twinkle—perhaps one of empathy—in his eyes.

"This is Kate Brown. We were just on our way out."

"Mr. Underhill, I've heard so much about you," I lied. On the contrary, in fact. Devin rarely talked about his father. Come to think of it, Devin and I hadn't talked about much of anything. I'd wanted to spend the evening with Fox, but when I turned to Devin to make the suggestion, he shifted restlessly from foot to foot.

"Well, I'd love to stay and chat, but Devin and I are going to be late for a concert," I begrudgingly fibbed. "I hope we can talk again soon." At least that part was truthful.

But "talking soon" never came. Unless soon was to-day, two years later. Looking at Fox now, it was apparent that he did not remember our first brief encounter, nor did I expect him to.

"Mr. Underhill, it's such a pleasure to meet you." I shook his hand. "We're all very eager to work on this account."

"The feeling is mutual, Ms. Brown," Fox said with a smile.

I seated myself next to Michael. "So, where's the man of the hour?" I asked Fox in what I hoped was a casual tone. Perhaps Devin had found out what Fox had planned for him and refused to show up. Then who would win the bet between Michael and me, I wondered? I frowned at myself. The last thing I needed was to get distracted. Focus on the task at hand, not the delicious food after said task at hand is completed.

"Devin's running late. Had some sort of appointment on the other side of the city, he tells me."

"Is he still unaware of the purpose of today's meeting?" Michael asked.

Fox nodded vigorously. "Definitely. I couldn't jeopardize that. This is too important to me."

I looked over at Gwen, whose grin reminded me of myself as a thirteen-year-old with a crush on Benji Waters. Man, did I love that boy, his oversized glasses and curly blond hair and all. Of course, Benji came out of the closet a decade later, but that was par for the course, I figured. I knew what that crush felt like sixteen years ago, and I was sure Gwen was going through the same thing right now. Perhaps Michael and I were right—Gwen had more invested in this account than just financial matters.

Michael must have noticed, too, and slightly nudged me. Without looking over, I acknowledged him with a slight tilt of my head.

"Let's talk briefly of your concern for your son's public image," Michael suggested to Fox. "Gwen filled Kate and me in this week, but we would love to get the full story from you."

Fox straightened his tie. "The company has been receiving complaints from family friends, who happen to be the biggest clients and supporters of Hotel Bella, about Devin's behavior."

"Could you be more specific? What do you mean by 'behavior?'" I inquired, even though all of us already knew the answer. This meeting was becoming a form of torture, with my asking questions that I didn't really want answers to.

"Within the last year or so, he has been out all night with some of New York's, uh, characters, and his encounters keep appearing in the press. Within the last few months, he has been coming to work late, blowing off meetings with investors, and refusing to talk to reporters about anything related to the company." Fox purposefully rolled back in his chair away from the table. "It might not seem to affect our hotels on an individual basis, but the overall image is declining. I'm sure you've seen the results of our last guest survey."

Gwen, Michael, and I nodded in unison. I pulled out a binder and spoke. "According to the survey, overall appeal of the hotel has dropped 22 percentage points since the last survey four years ago. That's a pretty big hit."

"Here's my question," Michael interjected. "We've all seen the articles and gossip columns and pictures of Devin's nightly exploits, but what makes you think that it's your son's after-hours reputation that's spoiling business for you, rather than the economy, or the general state of the world today?" Gwen shot me a panicked look, as if to say, "Shut him up! This isn't what I'm paying you guys for!"

"I think the latter and the former go hand in hand," stated Fox, unflappable. "Devin has decided to sow his wild oats in a time when the hotel business needs a level-headed leader more than ever. I'm not asking for perfection, just a better general image. And I don't care what needs to be done to reach that goal."

"Shall we launch into our plan, or do you want to wait for your son?" Michael asked.

Fox resituated himself in the black leather chair.

"Let's wait." Suddenly, the room fell silent. For the first time, Devin's absence became noticeable.

As she typically did, Gwen broke the silence. "Fox, I have a feeling that this cloudy morning is going to turn into a fabulous spring day! The smell in the air getting you excited for a summer in the Hamptons?"

"I feel like I'm getting too old for that scene," he said somewhat sternly. "I might just do some damage control at the individual hotels both nationally and internationally."

"You know, if you don't want your Hamptons home to be lonely, I could go there and keep it company." Gwen gave Fox an awkward, almost masculine, nudge, and they both laughed and continued talking of expensive summer homes.

Michael and I turned to each other and shared a questioning glance. He tapped my hand with his pen. "How you doing?" he asked softly. "Nervous?"

"Not until you reminded me." The acid crept slowly through my esophagus. Get here, Devin Underhill, so I can get on with my life.

My wish was answered. The four of us turned to the door to see Rita, our administrative assistant, escorting Devin into the conference room. She was in her early forties and had this weird half-smile on her face, which was the most emotion I had ever seen out of her. Yes, she must have been hypnotized by the Devin Underhill spell.

Meanwhile, I could feel my pulse throbbing in my neck. I swigged from my bottle of water, hoping it might slow down my heartbeat. Michael, Gwen, and I rose to greet Devin. His hair was a bit longer than it was two years ago, but everything else was the same: chiseled jaw, broad shoulders, and those eyes. I had to avoid those eyes. But they did seem to have slight bags under them, as if he had a rough night.

I took a deep, silent breath as I faced my past, looking sleek in his slate-gray suit. "Devin, Kate Brown. Pleasure to meet you."

This was the defining moment I had awaited for twenty-four hours, maybe longer. I saw the recognition in his eyes, those eyes I so wanted to avoid. Maybe I was lying to myself, but I thought I recognized a trace of happiness cross Devin's face. Or maybe it was more of a smirk.

We might have paused just a bit too long, since Michael came between the two of us and put out his hand. "Devin, Michael Korten."

"Michael Korten?" Devin repeated the name. "Say, did you happen to work with Derrik Train in L.A.?"

"As a matter of fact, I did. How do you know Derrik?"

"He's one of our best customers in Beverly Hills. He was having some troubles but really spoke highly of you and how you got him out of a few tough spots."

Weren't publicists at the bottom of the food chain? What Michael had done for Derrik was out of motivation for a hefty paycheck, I was certain, not to offer him a spiritual awakening.

"How is Derrik these days?" Michael dropped back into his chair. "I haven't talked to him since I left L.A. six months ago."

Devin shrugged. "Well, he's booked a hundred rooms

at the hotel next month for his 30th birthday." Michael plastered a smile.

"Needless to say," Devin continued, "I'm sure that I'll be pleased with your services just as Derrik has been."

Were Devin and Michael becoming fast friends? That figures.

"Let's see what happens," Michael said vaguely. "And maybe the most important person to know in this room is none other than Gwen Burton, CEO of this fine firm."

Gwen stood up and clumsily reached across the table for Devin's hand. "Oh, you're just like your father!" she exclaimed.

"Heh," Devin replied with a phony smile.

"Shall we get this meeting started?" Gwen suggested to no one in particular.

"Agreed," Devin replied. "My father never really told me why we're here. Would someone like to fill me in on the scope of this meeting?"

Gwen gleefully, almost maniacally, pointed to me. "I'll let Kate get us started, since she's still standing up. What say you, dear?"

I glanced at Michael, who shot back an encouraging smile. It was the least he could do, now that he and Devin were practically best buds. I grabbed large sheets of black foam core and walked to the front of the room.

I stood there, hands placed on my hips to look authoritative, but the real reason for putting them there was to keep me from tipping over. "Devin, have you taken a look at the Hotel Bella opinion survey from a few months ago?"

"Sure, I glanced over it, but I'm sure my father is disappointed that I didn't study it more thoroughly." Father and son exchanged a rancorous glance that made me feel uncomfortable.

"Let me fill you in on the highlights," I hastily continued, making a point to silently monitor my breathing. "The Hotel Bella image has been knocked down quite a few notches."

Devin leaned back in his chair and crossed his arms over his chest. "Isn't the entire hotel industry in this position? I'm not sure what you're getting at."

"From what we've been able to gather," I proceeded cautiously, "you seem to be getting some bad publicity."

Devin furrowed his brow. "Still not sure what you're trying to say."

"Do you read magazines? And do you know what they're saying about you? It's not pretty." I spoke directly.

Devin leaned back and locked his fingers behind his head. "This is rich." He cast a hostile eye toward his father. "Is this some sort of grand scheme to get me out of the company?" And then Devin returned his glance toward me, looking directly into my eyes. "Who doesn't like to have a good time every once in a while? I think your claim may be a tad exaggerated."

I'd hoped it wouldn't have come to this so soon, but I showed the group the first board. It contained about eight cutouts from magazines in which Devin had appeared in the last year. "Devin, in all of these, if you're not holding a woman, then you are holding a cigarette or a strong drink." I passed the board around the table. With a clenched jaw, Devin swept the board toward Fox without even looking at it, or his father.

"Of course, sometimes the New York media tend to catch celebrities at their worst moments." I put a spin on the situation, just as I had done for so many clients in the past. In fact, I was reveling in the moment more than I thought I would. Anna was right. I was one lucky girl to be in this position, deservedly putting an ex-boyfriend on the hot seat. "But this is eight inopportune moments."

"This feels like a trial," Devin complained.

"Stay with me. This isn't something that you're going to be tarred and feathered for. We feel that the guests of Hotel Bella are becoming turned off to a company once known for its strong family values that's now being led by a man who just doesn't seem to care who he's seen with or what he does in public."

Devin started standing up, but Michael put up a confident, reassuring hand.

"Devin, look, we're a PR firm, not the ethics police. Our job is to get Hotel Bella back on track, to get those profits up. And your father, well, all of us feel the best way to do so is to improve the public's perception of you."

Devin shot his father a baleful glance before turning back to Michael and me. "I'm not some sort of player," he said defensively. I saw the heat rise from his neck toward his forehead. Devin looked about two seconds away from a tantrum. I was going to win my bet with Michael.

Fox, who had been silent up to this point, spoke up. "Devin, do you really think this is a surprise? How many times have we talked about this? Your carousing is hurting business. Simple as that."

"Yeah, but did you really need to bring in a crack team of publicists?" Devin answered through clenched teeth.

"I need to know what your commitment is to this company, Devin. Are you in? Because if you're not, I'm ready to take it to the board."

Devin grasped the arms of the chair at the ultimatum from his father. I watched Michael, who eyed me with the same dumbfounded look I must have been wearing. Gwen's eyes were wide with excitement.

"Fine," Devin said abruptly. "Just tell me the plan."

I raised a suspicious eyebrow at Devin, who offered a slight nod. I cleared my throat. "As Michael said, we're not standing on a moral pedestal. We are just trying to make things easier for you, Fox, and the company. I have a feeling that your dedication and commitment to the family business trump the bad press." I tapped into my personal knowledge, rather than professional, of Devin to address that last issue. I hoped I had struck a nerve somewhere deep within Devin, since I was not confident whether I had believed my own words.

I chose to interpret Devin's silence as acceptance of my statement and introduced the plan. "Devin, this isn't as bad as it sounds. We're not asking you to cloister yourself. It simply comes down to common sense and timing. Who you're seen with, when you're seen with them, and what you're doing with them all matter."

I picked up a stack of bound presentations and distributed them. "You'll see that Michael and I have outlined some suggested hot spots, activities, and A-listers that'll all offer good press just by associating with them. Emceeing an auction with Rudy Giuliani, throwing out the first pitch at an all-star fund-raiser baseball game, showing up at hospitals for visits. Once you examine the lists, you'll notice that not much will change for you. Remember: common sense and timing. It's important to surround yourself with reputable, high-quality people."

With that, I seated myself at the table and nodded to Michael to describe the public relations makeover plan in detail. I needed a break. But I did it. I made it through the meeting with few flaws. The worst was over, or so I believed.

## Chapter Five

Had I misjudged Devin all along? I pondered, as I grabbed a bottle of water from the lunchroom. He'd withstood the criticism much better than I ever could have, and had even agreed with my and Michael's plan by the end of the two-hour meeting. On his way out of the conference room, Devin offered a genuine smile and a firm handshake. Michael, Devin, and I had agreed to regroup in a week to discuss plans in further detail; other than that, Devin said nothing else to me after the meeting.

Which was why I did a double take as I approached my office, where he was examining the photos on the wall.

I cleared my throat to announce my presence. Devin pointed to one of the pictures. "Who's the babe?"

"That babe is my friend Anna, whom you met many times while you and I were together." I made no attempt to hide my irritation.

"I was talking about you," Devin smirked. "That's a great picture. But why do I need to tell you how you look in a picture when I have the real thing in front of me?" Devin reached out for a hug, but I batted his arm away.

"You are a client. I don't hug clients."

"Kate, I just wanted to commend you on that performance in the conference room. I could tell that you were just in love with the idea that you could knock an old boyfriend down."

That was the first time Devin had ever acknowledged that he and I had ever dated. Throughout the relationship, Devin felt that labels were suffocating, so he maintained that what he and I were doing was simply two people having a good time together.

I challenged Devin. "What makes you so sure that what you saw in there was an act?"

"It just wasn't you."

"How exactly, Devin, would you know that was or wasn't me?" I nearly erupted. "For you to come here and say that I wasn't being myself is an insult that I don't want to hear. People change, Devin. I suggest you do the same."

Devin began to shake with laughter, which only annoyed me even more. "What's so funny?" I demanded.

He shook his head and wiped away a fake tear. "I was just playing with you. I was seeing if I could still get a rise out of you, and I certainly can. You're the same old spitfire I remember from a few years back. And by the way, it's sexier than ever."

Fortunately for me, his strong come-ons didn't affect me—much. Oh, it was certainly vintage Devin, thinking that he could throw out a few well-placed compliments and just watch me fawn after him at his feet. That's right, I needed to channel this disgust, if only to avoid getting hooked all over again. One thing I did know was that I needed to keep my physical distance from him, so I walked backwards toward an opposite corner of my office.

Devin's face suddenly became serious. "How have you been doing, Kate? I think about you a lot. When I saw you in the conference room, I just couldn't . . . you had me speechless, you know? For the last week, I've been racking my brain trying to figure out why Burton Relations sounded so familiar to me. Now I realize."

I heard nothing else after "I think about you a lot." That jerk. Nice of him to confess this after ignoring me for two years. Broken dates, I reminded myself. So considerate of him to tell me how fabulous and sexy I looked now, considering he hadn't said a peep about those things when we were dating. I was not about to get sucked into that trap again. I am a strong, professional woman, I am in touch with the world in which I live . . .

Forget all that, I thought. I was in touch with not letting a jerk like Devin rake me over the coals again. And forget about his sweet talk. We were here for work, and work we'd talk about. "Yes, I'm still at Burton Relations, obviously. I've had some great accounts—"

"And I suppose this one is the best?" Devin interrupted.

I attempted to decipher some sarcasm in his words. I stopped him, though, before he could speak any more.

"Devin, you may think that having you as a client is a gift from the heavens, but I have been and will continue to work as hard on this project as I do my others. I have faith that both you and I can put the past aside and handle this in the most professional way possible."

"If you think that *is* possible," Devin muttered.

"I know it is."

"So, are you seeing anyone?"

"What did I just say about keeping the personal separate from the professional?"

"Spoken like a true PR rep—avoid answering the tough questions. Let me try it again: Are you seeing anyone?"

Just as I opened my mouth for a flustered reply, Michael appeared at the door, his jacket strewn over his arm. He looked surprised. "Um, Kate, can you still make it to our lunch meeting?"

Lunch meeting. Code word for escape. I had almost forgotten. "I'll meet you at the elevator banks in five minutes," I told Michael.

Devin waited until Michael was out of earshot before speaking. "Forget about the last question. I already figured it out."

I frowned. "What's that supposed to mean?"

"Come on, Kate. He was practically salivating and panting!"

"Come on, Devin, I haven't seen you in two years and now you're asking me who I'm dating and making insinuations about my coworkers? Not that it's any of your business, but the same goes for him as it does for you or any other male who crosses my path in this job: I don't mix business with pleasure."

Devin was unconvinced. "Say what you will, but I have a pretty good idea what's going on in that head of yours."

I grabbed my purse and headed to the door. "Don't be so cocky. That's what got you in this office in the first place."

"How does this spot look?" Michael pulled out a chair for me and made sure I was seated before he sat down.

The restaurant was on the first floor of our building. Dangling blue and yellow light fixtures accented the mahogany bar area, while the dining area was more formal with white tablecloths and upholstered chairs. We were only one of six people in there, as most of the lunch crowd had already dissipated. Michael and I had each ordered a glass of champagne in celebration of our victory—or at least a first step on the road to what I hoped would be a victory, both personal and professional. Gwen surprised us by generously suggesting that we take the rest of the afternoon off. Then again, what she asked us to do in the last twenty-four hours was nothing short of turning water into wine.

I propped an elbow on the bar. "So, Michael, why, exactly, did you come to New York? Just a little too much sunshine out west for you?"

"It was probably the least calculated thing I did in my life," he admitted. "I don't know, one day I just felt that I owed it to myself to live someplace other than

Southern California. I mean, I was born and raised there—yes, it's true, there are a few of us like that out there—went to UCLA, got a job at a film studio right out of college, went into PR, and just wanted a change."

"No other catalyst?" I prodded.

He shifted. "Maybe."

"Was it a girl?" I asked pointedly.

"Yes, my ex-fiancée, to be specific." Suddenly he was intently focused on unwrapping the linen napkin holding the sterling silver flatware. I certainly didn't want to make the guy feel uncomfortable, but he quickly shook his head and snapped back to reality.

"We met at work. We'd been split up for about a year, but she and I were still working together, and I just thought, 'Michael, quit being an idiot and forcing yourself to face your ex every day.' So rather than looking for a new job in L.A., I used my connections to find something out here."

"And you found Gwen?" I was perplexed.

"It was kind of odd. Okay, *she* was kind of odd." Michael laughed as he traced the rim of his wine glass. "But despite her practically being a caricature, she was the only one who was upfront with me about what I'd be doing and what her mission was with her firm. And I had been with the big studios, the big publicity houses, my whole working life. Gwen was offering a competitive salary, I was willing to give the small firm a try, and here I sit, nearly a year later."

"So, was it everything you thought it would be?"

"Well, Gwen's a little crazier than I thought, but it's charming, in a twisted sort of way."

"Yes, it certainly takes a special breed to work with her."

"Yikes, what does that say about us?"

"That we love torturing ourselves?" I said dryly, as I reached for my glass of water.

"So, how did it end?"

"Pardon me?"

"How did it end with the fiancée?"

Michael grinned. "Oh, I see, you're using the same trick I used on you last night."

I shrugged. "I'm not above it. Seriously, though, no pressure if you don't want to talk about it."

"Well, without boring you with all the details, Jillian wanted her freedom, and she found that freedom with, oh, let's see, an actor, a director, and eventually our boss."

I wrinkled my nose. "Eww. What was your boss like?"

"Happy as a middle-aged clam once he got her into bed."

"And you worked with both of them for a year after that?"

"Makes you think twice about dating your coworkers." His eyes darted toward the back of the restaurant, while I wondered why his comment stung as much as it did.

He expertly covered up his comment. "You want to know how desperate I was to find an explanation for what went wrong? I actually bought *Men are from Mars, Women are from Venus.*"

"Wow, I've heard rumors that a man or two might have actually read that book. So," I asked him sheepishly, "did you see it on my bookshelf last night and you were just too put off to bring it up?"

"No, I didn't want to embarrass myself in front of you, but I might be doing that just now." He smiled, and for the first time, I noticed a dimple on his left cheek.

"You wanna talk about embarrassing? Once I worked out the nerves at our meeting, all I could think about was eating."

"I knew I'd win our little bet." Michael's eyes crinkled as he lifted his glass to his mouth. Much to my chagrin, I caught myself staring at his soft lips. "How does it feel eating crow?"

"Eating crow! That's something my mom would say."

"Oh, great, are you saying that I'm old and feminine?"

"No, just old." I winked.

"Do you even know how old I am?"

I offered a tongue-in-cheek guess. "Forty-nine."

Michael threw back his head and laughed. "Great guess. Try thirty-two."

"That's what I said. Thirty-two. When's your birthday?"

"March 9." Michael wrinkled his brow.

My lips curled. "Pisces."

"*Ding! Ding! Ding!*" Michael looked around. "If our waiter shows up, we'll have to ask him what fabulous prize our lovely contestant wins?"

I leaned over the table—had it just shrunk and brought us closer together?—and slugged Michael's tricep. Could he have been flexing just for me? "I'm a Cancer. Pisces make the best friends for us, or so the book *Lucky Stars* tells me. You probably saw that on the bookshelf, too." Was my low blood sugar clouding my thought process? Apparently our waiter had taken his lunch break.

"Yes, we are astrological matches. Quite compatible for each other." I wasn't quite sure if that's what he actually said, as my sights were elsewhere: watching the door, or more specifically, watching Devin exit.

Michael followed my gaze and his eyes cooled. "Was he here the whole time?"

"Nah. Just came in, scanned the place, and went away. I don't think he saw what he was looking for. Or maybe he saw us and scampered away. Like a scared little bunny."

"Why would he do that?"

"I'm telling you, the guy is one big puzzle."

"Do you think that's why women are drawn to him?" Michael sounded genuinely puzzled himself.

"Could be the supermodel good looks or the outrageous fortune, but sure, I suppose this air of mystery intrigues women."

"I've noticed that a lot about women, at least the ones I've dated," he amended. "The tougher a guy is to figure out, the more attracted they are to him."

I frowned, though I wasn't sure if it was because, on some level I knew he was right, and I didn't want to admit it.

Fortunately, I was spared a chance to respond, as our server finally arrived at the table, unapologetic for making us wait.

Michael gestured toward me, letting me order first. I realized that while I was feeling starved, I hadn't once opened the menu. When I did, I suddenly became self-conscious about what to order. Get over it, Kate, I said to myself. You're not on a first date. Don't be foolish—order what you want! "Chicken Caesar salad with dressing on the side," I ordered sheepishly.

Perplexed, Michael ordered steak tartare and a cold shrimp appetizer.

"I thought you were ravenous," he commented as the waiter walked away.

"Maybe the three sips of champagne have clouded my judgment," I unconvincingly offered.

"Cheap date." He smiled.

So I wasn't the only one who felt like we were on a date. Or maybe he was just being nice. Or maybe I didn't need to overanalyze it because this was strictly a business lunch.

I swiftly changed topics, a natural gift of mine. "What did you think of Fox?" I asked.

"He seems like a genuine guy." Michael nodded with pleasure in recalling the meeting. "And people around this city appear to think the same. Makes you wonder if Devin's trying to distance himself as far as possible from his perfect father."

"Try as we might, I believe we're destined to repeat our parents' patterns."

"I hope that's the case with me." I saw Michael's face soften for the first time. "My parents have been together for 35 years. When I was younger I was so embarrassed by their gushiness toward each other, but now, it's something that I really want for my own life, you know?" Michael paused, as if regretting what he said. He hastily changed the subject.

"So, have you been to this restaurant before?" he asked with no emotion.

And I thought Devin was a puzzle.

We shared idle chatter for about 10 minutes more before the food arrived. I picked at my salad, much like I picked at my food yesterday at the meal with Anna. What I needed was a hot pizza followed by a hot bath.

After the meal, I reached for my purse and pulled out a credit card. Michael reached across the table and gently pushed my hand away before searching through his own wallet.

"What are you doing?" I asked, the fatigue and poor nutrition from the last day finally catching up with me. "This was my bet, and I will make good on it."

"You didn't really think I was going to let you pay for this, did you?" The crease in Michael's head lessened. "Given what you've been through in the last twenty-four hours, I'd say that you're entitled to a free lunch, regardless of our silly little bet."

"Let me make you dinner some day."

Michael gave me an interested look and I suddenly panicked. Even though I was fatigued and famished beyond belief, I did not want to send the wrong signals. But what was right or wrong at this point? I couldn't determine how Michael interpreted my proposition. "Make you dinner" implied more than just a meal in a city where single men and women could barely tell the difference between the stove and the refrigerator. "I meant take you out for dinner," I backpedaled. "All in the name of business, you know. Because I am a cliché and can't cook." I squinted, trying to read Michael's expression.

Michael nodded halfheartedly. "Yeah, maybe sometime after work." He summoned the waiter so he could pay the bill.

I looked down and traced the condensation on the water glass, which sat next to my nearly full champagne glass and barely touched salad. My main concern now was getting into bed and sleeping. I glanced at my watch and noticed it was barely 3 P.M. What a lightweight.

Michael signed the receipt, walked to my side of the table, and offered me his arm. "Shall we?"

I accepted it graciously, taken aback by the gesture. The two of us exited the restaurant and waited on the curb for a taxi.

"How about we share the cab ride?" Michael suggested.

"Do you live by me?"

"No, but I want to be sure you make it home okay."

"It's daylight for at least another three hours. I'll be fine."

"I don't mind. You seem to have a hard time letting people do things for you, don't you?"

I had no energy to disagree, though I was sure the guilt would settle soon.

A cab pulled up, and Michael opened the door. I was silent for most of the ride; so was Michael. Lunch was a roller coaster of conversation: We went from jovial, borderline-flirtatious banter to awkward silence, and back and forth again.

The driver pulled to the sidewalk in front of my apartment. I dug in my purse, and again Michael offered to pay for the whole thing when he got home. "Thank you," I said benignly. "I'll see you tomorrow at work."

I hustled out of the cab, but not before Michael asked the driver to wait and make sure I safely entered the building.

I started to walk up the stairs when something commanded me to stop. Uncontrollably, I turned to look back at the cab. That's when I saw that Michael was only two feet behind me. Blood rushed to my face.

He feverishly rubbed his sideburn. "I, uh, just take it easy, and I'll see you tomorrow, all right?" He then awkwardly patted my shoulder and bounded down the stairs back to the cab.

Once in my apartment, the first order of business was to splash some cool water on my face, then to call Anna for help in dissecting the day's events. And of course, there was that pizza calling my name . . .

I walked toward the phone and noticed that the answering machine light was flashing. No need for voicemail in this household—nothing was as gratifying as a flashing light indicating someone wanted to talk to you, even if it was just someone trying to sell you new roofing or siding. I hit the button and heard that familiar voice.

"Kate, it's Devin. I saw you living it up with that Michael guy this afternoon. You were glowing." He chuckled slightly. "Well, I just wanted to say how great it was seeing you again today, and even though it's not a situation necessarily in my favor, I look forward to seeing more of you. Take care, babe."

"Ugh!" I screamed. I threw myself on the purple couch, and that's the last thing I remembered from this crazy day.

## Chapter Six

It was definitely getting too old for this, I thought as I punched the number twelve button on the elevator control panel. How could my beloved fellow New Yorkers stay up past 11 P.M. during the workweek? I had one stressful day, passed out before 6:00 P.M., and still could barely open my eyes enough to find my way to the bathroom, let alone to work. The elevator jolted when it stopped at Burton Relations, as did my stomach. I couldn't wait to tear into the bagel, muffin, and scone I had picked up on the way to work.

Oh, how easy it would have been to stay home. It made sense to not come in to work; I needed at least a day away from work to process the events of the previous twenty-four hours. And the fact that there's always some awkwardness the day after you go out for a work-but-not-really-work lunch with a single male coworker. You tend to open up about things that wouldn't have been said in an office setting, and then you obsess over whether you said too much or forgot that you might have said something incriminating. See, this is why I needed to go to work, despite whatever reaction I might get from Michael; I knew myself well enough that I would gradually become senile if I had that much time alone with my mind.

So I pulled myself out of bed, took a shower, brushed my teeth three times, threw on a pair of faded black trousers and a pale green sweater, and stumbled out the door without doing my hair or makeup. Or without my contacts, for that matter. My black-framed glasses with the scratched lenses and outdated prescription would have to suffice on a day in which I couldn't open my eyes more than a millimeter.

It was quite the contrast from yesterday's appearance—knowing my luck, this would be the day that a photographer from *Glamour* would snap my photo, only for it to appear in an issue with a black bar over my eyes under the "Fashion Don'ts" column.

I had three objectives when I got off the elevator: devour my carbohydrate breakfast of champions, wash it down with a pot of coffee, and stare blankly at my computer screen. I wanted to weep when I poured the first cup. Heading back toward my desk, I almost stumbled when I heard a distinctive female giggle coming from Michael's office.

Immediate curiosity struck, and I stuck my head out the door and sneakily peaked into his neighboring office through the crack where the door hinges meet the wall. There across from Michael sat an impossibly beautiful blond. She wore a simple white button-up shirt and red pants, yet she looked stunning. Michael presumably said something funny, because the woman giggled again with a toss of her silky, golden hair.

Who was she? She seemed so familiar. She certainly could not have been Michael's girlfriend—he'd never mentioned one before, and besides, she seemed too fun to be dating Michael. I hadn't heard about any new interns coming to work for us. I squinted through my glasses, trying to get a better look while keeping a low profile, but that didn't last for long.

"What, are you in cahoots with the paparazzi, Brown?" Gwen's shrill voice caused everyone within earshot to turn and look at me. "Why don't you just go in and talk to them, rather than longingly look at them from a distance? Hey, everyone, look! We have a Peeping Tammy right here in our office!" She laughed and walked off.

My face burning, I tried to pretend that I was looking for a file or a colleague or anything somewhat purposeful, but from the looks on their faces, I was pretty sure that Michael and the mystery woman knew that I was, in fact, a Peeping Tammy.

Michael stood up from his chair. "Kate, come on in, I want you to meet someone."

I was face to face with the blond, who was even more beautiful close up. She wore but a trace of makeup, yet she was flawlessly elegant. Despite the unflattering fluorescent lights overhead, her blue eyes still twinkled. How did I know this woman? Was she a former client? It hit me just as Michael was making his introductions.

"Kate Brown, Miranda Hamilton." He turned to Miranda. "Kate is one of our top execs." He then turned to me. "And Miranda is—"

"A real, live movie star, right here in our humble offices," I interrupted as I extended my hand for a shake. "It's great to meet you." That was one of my weakest salutations, I'll admit. I didn't know much about the "celebrity-types," as Gwen so affectionately called them, but Miranda was everywhere, and even I couldn't claim ignorance on this one.

"Well, thank you for the kind words." Miranda sounded genuine, but then again, she *was* an actress, I reminded myself.

"So, what brings you here?" Please don't say you're a client of Michael's, because Gwen will be so excited that she will quit today and hand the reins over to him, and poof, there goes my promotion.

"Actually, I'm in town about to start a shoot. Michael is an old friend from his days in L.A., so I decided to pop in for a little visit." She turned to Michael, who beamed with pride.

What was with all the "old friends" that kept appearing in our office? First Fox Underhill, now Miranda Hamilton?

The three of us stood in silence for a moment. "Well, I should get back to work, or at least start work. Late morning, I guess." I stumbled through my words.

"Oh, yes, Michael filled me in on the shenanigans of yesterday afternoon."

My head snapped toward Michael, who was tracing a sheet of paper on his desk. I could not believe it—he's telling someone who's a complete stranger to me about who knows what. I continued to stare at him, and he continued to awkwardly trace. "All good things, don't worry," Miranda smiled brightly at me, as if reading my thoughts. "Listen, Kate, would you like to join Michael and me for lunch?"

"I'd love to, but I have a Hot Pocket in the freezer that's been loyally waiting for me the past few days."

"Well, then, I insist that both of you join me for dinner tomorrow night."

"We can't," Michael spoke. "We have another event to cover."

We did, indeed—our first outing with Devin, a fundraiser for a children's cancer hospital.

"Then we definitely have to work something else out," Miranda said cheerfully.

"Definitely," I mimicked. If nothing else about my job, I have learned to read all the niceties that go along with the business.

Excusing myself, I went back to my office and immediately dialed Anna's cell. "Hey, it's me. You busy?"

"No, but in a little while I'm actually heading to Bloomie's for a launch of a new makeup line. What's up?"

"Tell me what you know about Miranda Hamilton."

"Miranda Hamilton? I hear she's great!" Anna practically cooed. "I guess she used to do Broadway here occasionally, and this city just loves her. Hollywood loves her, the public loves her. She just seems really down to earth, from what I hear and read."

"Well, then, you'll be happy to hear that I met her today."

"No way!" Anna sounded like a thirteen-year-old girl who just saw the New Kids on the Block centerfold in *Tiger Beat*. "How? How did you meet her? I am doing my best to disguise my envy, you know."

"She actually is in the office right now. She's meeting with Michael—an 'old friend' from Los Angeles."

"Uh-huh," Anna said knowingly. "Old friend. We know what that means."

"Exactly what I was thinking. I want to know how Michael dated someone like her. Okay, so he isn't *that* bad-looking, but come on."

Anna chuckled. "Ooh, somebody's jealous!"

"You've got to be kidding!" I fired back.

"Then why do you even care what their relationship is?"

"I don't. It's just that . . ."

"It's just that, what?" Anna challenged me.

"It's just that I don't get it, and I don't like it when I don't get it."

"Whatever you need to tell yourself," Anna mumbled.

"I heard that!"

"So, would it be in poor taste for me to ask you to introduce me to her?"

This is where Anna and I greatly varied. She was star-struck—she got her sticky little paws on every tabloid and magazine that mentioned any sort of celebrity. I, on the other hand, never enjoyed that scene, despite the fact that my career sometimes put me in those situations. "She invited me out to dinner with her and Michael tomorrow night."

"Ohmigod! You're going, right?"

"A, Michael and I have to do a Devin thing, and B, she didn't mean it—my guess is that famous people just say that stuff to make the common folk feel special. However—and this is a big however—if she *does* happen to shatter the mold and follow through, then you should go in my stead."

"Woo-hoo!" Anna shrieked. "I owe you big time."

"Eh," I shrugged. "I should get started on work."

"Good luck with your new best friend. I'll call to check in later."

I hung up the phone and watched through the doorway of my office as Miranda parted ways with Michael and gave Gwen a big hug good-bye, despite the fact that the two had presumably just met. Maybe Anna was right—this might be someone who lived up to the favorable reputation the press has provided. And she was more than nice to me, even after she found out from Michael about yesterday afternoon. What exactly did he tell her, anyway? All good things, she said. Huh. I wonder what that meant. Not that I care or anything.

## Chapter Seven

"**O**n behalf of Hotel Bella, Inc., I present the Children's Cancer Center with this check for $10,000." Turning to smile for the cameras, Devin handed the check to the surprised chair of the event. He received a standing ovation as he posed for pictures with the event co-chairs and cancer survivors with whom he shared the stage.

I leaned over to Michael, who was standing next to me in the back of the banquet room where this fundraiser was taking place. "Devin genuinely seems to enjoy being here," I murmured.

"The event isn't done yet," he said with a raised tone.

"I don't think it would hurt to cut him some slack."

Michael raised an eyebrow. "Why the sudden change of heart?"

I looked at him skeptically. "What do you mean?"

"You didn't seem to be his biggest fan as of two days ago, that's all."

Wow, working with Devin was making me testier than I realized. "Look, if we're not optimistic about the potential for this personality transformation, then others—particularly the press—could pick up on it. Besides, it's all I can do to talk myself into it, so just play along."

Michael nodded. "You're right, you're right. I apologize. I'm just a little edgy today."

"Why's that?"

"Oh, Miranda and I were up most of the night catching up." My heart leapt, but I ignored it. Why should I care that "old friends" were catching up? "She really liked you."

"Why? Was it the bad hair, the archaic outfit, or the crooked eyeglasses?"

Michael gave a half-grin. "Don't worry about it. You looked good. No, she was really sincere about doing dinner tonight. Since we couldn't go to dinner, she wants us to get together with her afterward."

I looked up at the stage, where Devin was still schmoozing. "What about him? Don't you think we should keep an eye on him after the event? I am willing to hang around if you want to do the party thing with Miranda."

"I don't think that's a good idea, the two of you alone," Michael said hastily. He must have seen the perturbed look on my face, because he recanted. "I didn't mean it like that. Since he still has that lounge lizard thing going on, I wouldn't want you to have to try to rein him in. It wouldn't be fair to you. Why don't we talk him into coming along with us? That way we can still have some fun and keep him in our sights."

Oh, yes, that's how I wanted to spend a Friday night: surrounded by an ex-boyfriend, a colleague, and a gorgeous actress.

The crowd at the fund-raiser started to dissipate. "So, did I meet your approval?" Devin winked at me and outwardly ignored Michael's presence.

"Yes. In fact, you seemed to really enjoy yourself up there."

"Whatever," Devin said flippantly. "Just get me out of this monkey suit so I can get on with my weekend."

I pulled Devin aside. "Hey, I thought that you were on board with the changes we had discussed earlier this week."

"I am. That doesn't mean I can't go out and party a little bit, does it?"

"It's this kind of attitude that is unacceptable. And by the way, it's really starting to annoy me," I said in a loud whisper.

Devin smirked and squeezed my shoulder. "Whatever you say. You're the boss." I caught Michael rolling his eyes. He stepped over to us.

"Devin, Kate and I are going to a private party, and we think you should come with us."

"Yawn." He fiddled with his cuff links. "Sounds like a lot of shuffleboard and cribbage."

"Believe it or not, it's a cast party. Miranda Hamilton will be there," Michael said nonchalantly.

Devin slowly nodded as a sly grin spread across his face. "I could do that."

"Hmph!" I said a little louder than I wanted to. Both Devin and Michael looked at me, then turned back to each other.

"You know, it's only about ten blocks from here. Want to walk with us?" Michael suggested.

"Well, I really don't want to wear this out on the town," Devin said as he looked at his suit, "but if it means getting to a hottie like Miranda Hamilton a little sooner, then yes, I'll go."

We exited the event center and headed toward the party. I purposely fell behind Devin and brought Michael with me so we could talk.

"Why did you throw Miranda out there like bait?" I asked him. "Isn't this a little counterproductive?"

"It worked, didn't it? Trust me, she won't be interested in him."

"Why? Is she seeing someone?" I tried to act casual.

"Nah, I don't think so. But I guarantee that Devin is not Miranda's type."

Lux, the bar that was hosting the party, was quintessential New York: good fashion (lots of tight-fitting shirts on both the men and the women), good music (a DJ in the middle of the dance floor spinning techno beats), great-looking people (need I say more?). The tall, midnight-blue booths and opaque tabletops were part old-school diner, part *The Jetsons*. From the moment I walked in, I feared that we had brought Devin into his personal Mecca, but Michael assured me that it would be fine, as long as we were on our toes. On our toes. Easy for him to say. I did not have a good feeling about the evening, and all I wanted to do was go home, put on my robe, and watch some Friday-night stand-up comedy on TV.

I had called Anna on our way to the bar to invite her along, so I kept one eye on the door and another on Devin, since Michael had left to find Miranda. Devin and I found a spot at one of bars. He bought me a gin and tonic, but I refused. "Sorry, can't drink. I'm on the clock."

"Hey, how come you never returned my message? Couldn't pry yourself off of Lover Boy?"

My jaw tightened. "Why do you care? Not that I even owe you an explanation, but he and I are as platonic as you and I are."

"Is that how you describe us, platonic?" Devin spoke methodically, as if he were doing a guest spot on a soap opera. Thankfully, I saw Anna enter the party; I had never been so excited to see her. I waved her over.

She didn't even acknowledge Devin's presence, which made me gleeful. I heard Michael shouting my name over the house music. I turned to see Miranda, wearing a black strapless minidress with black Jimmy Choos with four-inch heels, at least. Before I could even react, Miranda walked up and gave me a hug. "It's so good to see you again, Kate! You look fantastic."

Glad somebody noticed. I wore a cropped black blazer over a black and purple off-the-shoulder top, which sat right at the waistband of my black hip-huggers. The outfit had been in my closet for six months, just waiting for its debut.

Miranda was starting to grow on me, if only for her ability to improve my self-esteem. "Miranda, this is my best friend, Anna. She's a makeup artist."

Miranda and Anna shook hands. "I bet we have a lot of stories between the two of us," Miranda grinned. "We'll have to swap tales later tonight. I have to make the obligatory rounds first."

Anna said nothing, just beamed. She loved the energy of the dark, loud bars, and couple that with the fact that she got to hang out with Miranda Hamilton—well, I certainly earned my friendship badge for the evening.

Miranda turned to the group. "Hey, everyone, we have a VIP room in the very back of the bar. The bouncers are expecting all of you, so you shouldn't get any flack. I'll be there in a few minutes."

Before she left, Devin stepped forward. "We haven't met yet. I'm Devin Underhill, and I must say, I am a huge fan of yours."

Miranda shrugged her shoulders and smiled. "Thanks!" was all she said. As she exited, her hips swayed as she made her way through the crowd, stopping every five seconds to chat someone up. I could see Devin staring after her.

"Someone should give him a hankie to wipe his drool," Anna said under her breath.

"I must talk to her more." He slowly followed her, enchanted.

I quickly pivoted toward Michael. "You've created

this beast, now you're going to have to tame him. I knew this wasn't a good idea."

Michael, too, looked worried, but he tried to sound composed. "I'll follow him, distract him somehow."

It was just Anna and I left. "So, should we go claim our VIP status while we have the chance?" I asked her.

"I've never been a VIP before. And to be one with Miranda Hamilton is even better. See, I told you that she was sweet!"

"Yeah, she isn't as bad as I thought," I reluctantly admitted.

The entrance to the VIP room was cloaked in a black velvety drape. The security guard pushed it aside for us, introducing three dark-blue leather couches formed in a horseshoe shape, an aquarium with exotic fish, and a glass coffee table lined with every kind of liquor imaginable. The sunshine-yellow walls were a bright (and surprising) contrast to the rest of the bar, though they were somewhat muted by the faint light coming from the green-fringed lamps.

The lounge was a peaceful oasis from the chaotic bar scene. The house music was muted, and patchouli candles gave the air a hearty, musky scent.

I looked around and saw about a dozen important-looking people, some of whom were obvious trendsetters and probably paid to just stand there and look cool, others still in business suits. I leaned toward Anna. "Any of those people look familiar?"

She casually scanned the crowd and tapped her chin. "Hmm. I think I worked with one of those guys on a play a few months ago. I'll be right back." Within seconds, Anna was being swept off her feet by a chiseled He-Man. While they hugged and gushed how great the other one looked, my eyes wandered around the room. Here I was, the PR woman, the one who makes things happen, cha, cha, cha, and I was all alone. How did this happen?

I begrudgingly wandered back into the bar, pretending that I was important, or at least looking for someone important. Then Michael appeared about six inches from my face.

"Hi," he smiled. "Having fun?"

"Sure, until I was left all alone in the VIP room." I stuck out my lower lip and quivered mockingly.

"There, there," Michael patted my shoulder. "Devin ran to get a drink, so I'm just keeping my eye out for him." He scanned the crowd. "Man, I just cannot relate to him."

I raised an eyebrow. "What do you mean?"

"I've tried to make conversation, and his eyes keep wandering to the next woman who walks past. He doesn't listen, doesn't have much of an attention span. He's like a five-year-old."

"And he wonders why we have to 'publicly babysit' him," I bemoaned. "I was just on my way to the ladies' room, so I'll send him your way if I see him."

I made my way through the throes of people crowding the dance floor. At the edge, about 20 feet ahead of me, I saw Devin grabbing an unsuspecting Miranda by her waist as she walked by.

He stood about a foot taller than she, even in her heels. He leaned over to say something in her ear, and she smiled and dismissed herself. But he wasn't giving up. He whispered something again in her ear, and she laughed politely. She looked like she was trying to get away, but even Miranda Hamilton might have gotten caught up in Devin Underhill's charisma.

I frantically looked behind me for Michael, hoping he might be witnessing this, but he was out of sight. I started to march over to the pair to pull them apart when something even more severe caught my eye. Randall Steck, a pencil-necked tabloid photographer privy to many moments of celebrities behaving badly, was gearing up to take a shot of Devin and Miranda. Sure, it was obvious that she didn't want to be here, but the cameras are unforgiving; it only takes a second or two of any sort of intimate contact, and poof, you're in tomorrow's rags. This was the last thing I needed to happen. I hustled to Randall and tapped him on the shoulder. He ignored me. So I stepped in front of his camera. "Hey, lady, get out of my way!" he sneered.

"Randall," I said pleadingly.

He slowly moved his camera to the side and looked at me quizzically. "Do I know you?"

"Probably not, but I know you, or at least of you, and I am begging you not to take this picture."

"Sure, I'll just close up shop and tell my boss that some dame told me I couldn't take my photos, so I just left."

Dame? Well, at least I wasn't a broad. He set up his shot again, but I didn't budge. "Look, you need to get out of my way," he nearly howled.

I began chewing on my lower lip. Think, Brown,

think. Time slowed as my head turned from Devin, who was on the verge of going in for a kiss with Miranda, to the photographer. Just as I saw Randall about to make that fateful click, I stepped behind Devin and Miranda, squeezed in between them, threw my arms around their shoulders, and offered my best, broadest grin at the moment the flash lit up the room.

Randall shook his head in disgust at the missed photo op and sauntered to another area of the party.

Devin and Miranda both stepped back. He stared at me, while she stepped aside. "Care to explain that one, Kate?" Devin's arms were tightly folded across his chest.

"Remember that meeting a few days ago where we talked about this very thing? There was a tabloid photographer over there. So the only thing I could think of doing was showing up in the picture with you and Miranda since it wouldn't be of any value to the papers with me in it."

"So, it bothered you that much that I was dancing with someone else, huh?" Devin's lips snarled into a mocking grin.

"Let's see, I could keep my job, or I could get jealous of a boy behaving badly."

Devin looked at me and could only muster a weak shake of his head. He disappeared into the crowd, and I turned to where Miranda was standing, and she, too, had disappeared. Maybe they were heading to his townhouse, and then the AP would pick up on this sordid affair, and I would be out of a career. No, no, I mustn't think like that. I've been in situations where my girl-friends and I have been trapped at bars talking to men we don't want to be talking to, and we've all had that look that Miranda had.

I sucked in my breath and marched through the bar hoping to find Anna, or even Michael. But I kept one eye open for Devin, too, just in case he didn't make it past the front door. I wandered back to the VIP room, where I saw Anna, Michael, and Miranda laughing and sharing stories. I motioned for Michael to come chat with me.

"Don't worry, he caught a cab home," Michael said.

"How did you know I—"

"Miranda told me about the situation on the dance floor. She found me, and I found him. He said he was tired and was just going home."

"You believed him?" I panicked.

"My guess is that it was a matter of pride, so it was better for him to just leave. Trust me, it's a guy thing."

Miranda and Anna had joined us. "Look, Kate, Michael filled me in on this Devin situation, and I am so sorry for doing anything to jeopardize your work."

"Don't worry, you're not the one at fault here. I saw the whole thing happen. And I'm sorry for, um, interrupting the photo op."

Miranda threw back her luscious blond mane and laughed heartily. "Are you kidding? Thank you for doing that! Devin seems okay, but I just am not into guys who are so forward like that. You know, the ones who try too hard?" She hooked her arm through Michael's and beamed at him.

I looked away, trying to hide my surprise. Maybe they were an item after all, but really, it wasn't any of my business, I assured myself. And despite her best intentions, Miranda was a wild card. Sure, she was nice, even sincere, but my big concern was to get Devin on the straight and narrow, and Miranda Hamilton was a major distraction. I just needed to find a way to approach the subject ever-so-delicately with Michael.

## Chapter Eight

"Can I come in?" I had tapped on Michael's office door and waited in the doorframe.

"Sure. I was just going to stop in your office to discuss our schedule with Devin. Between the fund-raisers for the youth groups and the charity golf tournaments next month, all his free time will be controlled by us."

"Well, that's part of what I wanted to discuss with you. Some of it has to do with the other night at Lux."

Michael raised his eyebrows. "Oh, yeah, pretty crazy, huh? I'd say we—really, you—were pretty successful, seeing that Devin went home alone in a cab."

I pursed my lips and shifted them to the side. This was going to be harder than I thought. "There's more," I blurted.

Michael's phone rang. "Sorry, I should take this. Hold on a moment." He picked up the receiver. "Michael Korten." Pause. "Hey, M. Can I call you back?

I'm in a meeting right now." He paused again. "Yeah, she's right here." Another pause. "Sure, I'll tell her."

M . . . as in Miranda. And they were talking about me. No need to be paranoid, right? Right?

Michael put the phone in his cradle and gave me a smirk. "I think someone is taken with you."

"Eh?"

"That was Miranda, and she wants to take you out to dinner to make up for that whole photography mishap with Devin the other night. She thinks you're pretty cool and can't stop talking about you."

I furrowed my brow. "Hmm, a female celebrity is taken with me."

Michael laughed. "No, she just thinks you're so real, and she doesn't get that in Hollywood all that much. Kind of makes her miss the old days."

"She barely knows me."

"Nah, I've known her practically my whole life, and she has a good read on people."

Great. Childhood sweethearts. Old friends, I reminded myself. They probably made a cheesy pact when they were 21 that if they were still single at age 35, they'd marry each other. At the very least, maybe she'd ask me to be a bridesmaid.

I checked back into the present. "Well, I'm pretty busy with work and all, so I don't know if dinner will work anytime soon."

"How about tonight? She and I already had plans to go out after she wraps her shoot for the day."

I shook my head and gave a halfhearted smile. "Hey, Korten, did you not hear me? I'm busy."

"On a Tuesday night? Come on. It'll be fun. There's nothing planned for Devin tonight. Might as well enjoy the time away from him while we've got it. What else have you got going on?"

Um, for starters, there were three separate reality shows on three separate stations that I had to try to schedule in. And that pint of chocolate Häagen Dazs in the freezer was not going to eat itself. And let's not forget staring at the wall occasionally, wondering how Miranda kept track of all the men that fell under her spell.

Michael smiled, and I noticed for the first time his perfectly straight grin. "It's like I see the hamster working up there," he tapped my head lightly, "trying to come up with an excuse."

"Can I bring Anna?"

"Absolutely. It'll be just like at the Lux, except no Devin."

"Except no Devin," I mindlessly repeated. Although I heard it as "Accept No Devin."

"All right, you've worked your publicist's magic and have convinced me to go." Perhaps it was all the compliments showered upon me by Miranda, or the fact that I was going to get a free dinner, but I actually looked forward to kicking back with some new friends.

"Ohmigod, ohmigod, ohmigod!" Anna squealed and jumped up and down. The bathroom attendant looked away and pretended she wasn't listening to us.

"We're out of earshot now, so can you tell me why you dragged me to the bathroom?"

"Miranda has asked me to come on board as a makeup artist on her new film."

I let out a whoop. "Anna, I am so proud of you! Is that what you and Miranda were being so secretive about out there?"

"I wouldn't say secretive, but I don't think she wanted to announce it to the entire restaurant."

"When do you start, my famous makeup artist friend?"

"Tomorrow, 6 A.M."

"Ouch. Does Miranda know that's when you usually go to bed?"

Anna gave me a playful slap on the hand. "Hush, you. I'm like a little kid hopped up on Pixie Sticks on Christmas Eve. Like I'm even gonna sleep!"

"This is huge. We should probably get back out there and celebrate—and finish our appetizers, of course."

"Can you call them appetizers in a place like this?" Anna teased as she pulled open the restroom door adorned with multicolored geometric patterns.

Mod was the name of the place we were at tonight. Last week it was Lux. Apparently giving monosyllabic titles to hot spots was hip. Another monosyllabic word. And probably a name already taken for the next big hangout.

I turned back toward Anna as we trudged through a long, narrow walkway flanked by high-top avocado-green tables. Unfortunately, she stopped while she squinted at our table, and I smacked into her. "Hey, chica, are you trying to knock me unconscious? Must we review the single-file protocol again?" I giggled, but Anna continued to look at our table, appearing distraught. I followed her gaze and saw that Devin was standing at the table talking with Miranda and Michael.

He turned to see me. I tilted my head and gave a "You've got to be kidding me" look. "It's great to see you too, Kate!" Devin enunciated condescendingly.

"How about if we take a walk, Devin?" I faked politeness and turned to walk toward the bar.

I didn't have to turn around to know that Devin had followed me. We got to the bar, in all of its '70s faux retro glory, complete with wood paneling behind the bartender. I quickly snapped my head. "So, Devin, I suppose you just happened to be here for another engagement, and you just conveniently ran into Miranda."

He shrugged. "Something like that."

"Now why don't you tell me the real story."

"And have you blow my cover?"

"My apologies, double-0-7."

"I had to see her again. Something about her . . ." He sucked in a breath through his teeth. "Man."

I rolled my eyes. "Ugh, please don't talk to me like I'm one of your buddies." I looked him up and down. "Wow, you're pretty brave, coming back after getting rejected not that long ago."

"Might I remind you, she didn't reject me Katherine. You happened to get in our way, and she disappeared. Probably thought you were a lunatic the way you jumped in between us."

"As a matter of fact, she invited me to dinner tonight," I huffed.

"Has she said anything about me?" Trying to appear nonchalant but really looking nonplussed, Devin thrust his hands into his pockets.

"Let's find out. Just let me write on this napkin, 'Do you like Devin? Check a box, yes or no.' "

He nodded toward the general direction of the table, which was out of sight from our standpoint. "Hook me up."

"Pardon?"

"Since you two are such great friends, you could put in a good word for me."

"Do you hear yourself? I am getting paid to do damage control for you. I am not going to play matchmaker for you with a Hollywood star."

"Fine, I'll just do it myself. I've always done it that way, and it's always worked for me." He winked and walked back to the table.

I sipped on a Diet Coke, trying to collect my thoughts, when I felt a tap on my shoulder. Michael.

"So, do I dare ask what he's doing here?"

"I think you know."

"Well, either he's really interested in Miranda, or he's really interested in me."

I managed a laugh through my exasperation. "You were right what you said about Devin the other night at Lux. He is a brat. Like a naughty, naughty kid who won't listen to anyone in a position of authority."

"Hey, don't stress over something you can't control." Michael gave me a gentle rub between my shoulder blades, which made my stomach flip. "You're doing a great job with him."

"Thanks, but I feel like I'm pedaling backward."

"Sounds like something Ralphie Wiggum would say."

"He's my favorite character on *The Simpsons*."

"Hey, mine, too! Favorite Ralph line?"

" 'Me fail English? That's unpossible!' Yours?"

" 'Doctor told me that *both* my eyes were lazy! And that's why it was the best summer ever.' "

I clutched my stomach with laughter. "You see, *The Simpsons* is not only a cultural icon, but it brings the masses together."

Michael set down his glass. "You're the first woman I've met who really appreciates *The Simpsons*. I mean, I've known plenty of women who have watched the show, but watching it and appreciating it are two different things."

"You mean all the women in your life don't do horrible impressions of animated characters? You should ask Anna to do her impression of Moe."

"Yikes, I don't know if I want to see—or hear—that."

"And you think I enjoy it every time she breaks it out?"

More laughter from Michael. And a quick brush of his hand on my arm. He awkwardly and hastily retracted his hand. "Woops," was all he could muster.

I pushed my stool back. "I should check on the lovebirds before they start making a nest."

"Miranda isn't the one you have to worry about here." Michael said confidently. "She has no interest in Devin whatsoever."

I eyed Michael suspiciously. "How do you know?"

"I just do." He zoned out while I tried to define his relationship with Miranda. College roommates, maybe? Old family friends? Of course, I could always just ask. But that was not my concern now. I needed to keep my eyes on the prize—if that was what you could even call Devin. Michael walked a few paces ahead of me back to the table, where we saw Miranda and Anna laughing heartily and Devin sitting at the edge of the table with his back turned slightly toward them. He was noticeably pouting.

"Uh, oh, are the popular kids ignoring you?" I slid in the chair next to him.

"I haven't gotten a word in edgewise. It's like I'm not even here."

"Watch out when the girls get together. You'll be sitting there by yourself for a long time."

"Where were you, making out with Michael?"

I looked down at myself mockingly. "Oops, my shirt's on backwards!"

Devin nodded toward Michael, who had moved in closely toward Miranda. His arm was on the back of her chair, and unlike Devin, he was able to leap into the conversation and laugh. He looked at Miranda with a sense of—a sense of—pride, perhaps? It wasn't quite lust, but it wasn't quite a look you'd get from someone who's just a friend, either.

"Look at us, pining for people who don't want us," Devin leaned close to me and spoke in a muted tone.

I tossed my head toward Devin. "I'm not pining."

He ignored my comment. "Well, you go ahead and stare all you want, but I'm doing something about it."

"Devin, don't get stupid."

"Don't worry, all right? I've been on my best behavior tonight. Only one cameraman came over, and he took a very politically-correct shot of me and Miranda and Anna. Look, just because I'm under your care doesn't mean I can't date."

"I hate to break it to you," I tried to keep my voice down so the rest of the table wouldn't hear, "but I don't think Miranda's interested."

"I've barely gotten a chance to know her. And you know me, I don't give up that easily."

"Only when it benefits you," I mumbled, recalling our own breakup. Very clean and easy for him. He'd had his assistant do it. There's rejection, and then there's rejection via your boyfriend's sixty-year-old temporary assistant. I had called Devin's office wondering what we had planned for that night, and Maria answered his line.

"Oh, Mr. Underhill wanted me to pass a message on to you. It's Katie, right?"

"Kate," I replied curtly.

"Anyway, he just doesn't think it's going to work out and thinks it best you go your separate ways. Good-bye."

Yes, very clean and easy. And as I watched him watching Miranda, I knew that he wouldn't give up on her easily.

I caught Michael's eye. He nodded toward the front door. He dismissed himself from the table, and I followed about five seconds later.

Michael was standing outside with his hands thrust deep into his pockets, shifting from one foot to another, when I slid up next to him. I don't know if it was

Michael or someone else walking by, but I caught a whiff of a spicy cologne. Mmm.

"Can't take the New York winter?" I teased.

"These are the times I really miss L.A."

I deeply inhaled the crisp March air. "What, and give up all the damp, dreary, drizzly days of early spring in Manhattan?"

"Uh, oh, it's come to this. We've resorted to talking about the weather." He gave me a halfhearted smile.

"So, was there something you wanted to talk to me about?" I encouraged.

He reached a hand up to his sideburn and started absently rubbing it. "Uh, just curious about what you and Devin were talking about."

"I think he's obsessed with Miranda. I mean, I know Devin intentionally showed up tonight, but I, er, well, maybe . . ." I stumbled through my words, remembering what I wanted to talk to Michael about earlier today.

Michael raised his eyebrows encouragingly. When I opened my mouth to say that I don't think we should be hanging around Miranda, I realized that she was not the problem here. "It's, it's . . . it's not important."

Michael looked down at the sidewalk and traced a half-circle with his shoe. "It's not that you want to get back together with Devin, is it?" he said rather abruptly.

"Phawww!" I guffawed. "You know, the more time I spend with that man, the less attractive—and redeeming—he becomes."

"Well, that's good news." He stared intently at me. I

felt heat come to my cheeks, so I had to look away. "Um, we should get back inside."

And suddenly he had darted back into the restaurant, leaving me alone to wonder what just happened.

## Chapter Nine

It had been a lovely two weeks. It was mid-April, there were hints of buds on the trees, and I had been given an emergency project with another client that was just wrapping up that day, so Michael was the one accompanying Devin to his events.

I felt a twinge of guilt, making Michael do all the physical labor on this project. But I did what I could during bouts of quiet time with my other project. I called reporters and schmoozed the best I could about why they should be interviewing Devin Underhill about his new commitment to charity. It was no easy task, having the phone slammed down in your ear an average of five times a day—but I'd take it over spending any time with Devin. I knew I'd have to buck up pretty soon, but right now I was basking in the moment.

And what a brief moment it was. Michael entered

my office unannounced. "Hey, you're finishing up the Mason account today, right?"

Here we go. "Unfortunately, yes. I'm guessing my shift is starting up again with Devin?"

"You guess right, but we can talk about that later. About what time will you be available today? Maybe noon?" He grinned mischievously.

I watched him skeptically. "Depends on what you want me to do."

"Play hooky and come with me to a baseball game." I thought he was dressed a little casually today, with his baby-blue button-up shirt and khakis.

I wrinkled my nose. "Is it a Yankees game?"

"Like I'm that well connected. It's Mets vs. the Brewers."

"Yay, I love the Mets!" To my chagrin, I sounded like an overly enthusiastic cheerleader.

"All right, game time is at 1:00, but we should leave at 11:00 if we want to even consider being there on time."

"What happened to noon?"

"You're pedantic."

"Ooh, big college word," I teased, and I saw him soften a little. Ever since the night at the restaurant, communication had been perfunctory. He'd only stop by when he had a question about Devin, and nothing else. I had been so wrapped up in my other account that fortunately, I hadn't really noticed. Maybe some over-priced stadium dogs would do us some good.

"What about Gwen?"

"She's out of the office the rest of the day. If she asks, we'll just say we were out doing 'research.' Anyway, I should let you finish your work." Michael pivoted to make an exit. "So, we've agreed upon 11:00?"

"Tricky like a good old-fashioned publicist, just spinning the conversation right around like that." I smiled and nodded. "Yes, 11:00 should work."

"You better be nice to He Who Holds The Tickets."

"How dare you hold that over me!" I mockingly cried.

Michael glanced at his watch. "It's 10:00 already. Why don't we just leave now and grab an early lunch first?"

"And not be given the chance to eat my weight in hot dogs? I don't think so."

"All right, I'll let you get back to business so you can cram an entire day's worth of work into an hour." Michael left the office and was back in ten seconds. "Can we go yet?"

I shooed him away. "Don't tempt me. I'm very fragile when it comes to my Mets."

"You're right, you're right. I'll let you continue your work." And he reappeared another ten seconds later. "How about now?"

"Michael! Naughty! Go to your room!" He purposely shuffled out of the office as I grinned into my paperwork. I made a few phone calls, sent out a press release, and shuffled papers around my desk to make it look like I was returning after the game. Michael again came into my office. "For real this time, can we go?"

I looked at the clock on my wall. "11:00 sharp. You're good. Are we taking the subway?"

"No, I drove in today."

Hmm, he owned a car and was able to pay for parking. Yup, he was definitely making more than me. We walked about six blocks to a lot in which all the cars were crammed. He led me to his vehicle and unlocked the door for me. I opened the door and had about three inches of room to slither in.

"So this is what a car looks like." Granted, it was a 1996 silver BMW, but it was a BMW nevertheless. "You realize I'm doing my best to refrain from Wall Street yuppie jokes, right?"

Michael shook his head and laughed.

I looked around at the spotless leather interior. "Ever since I got my driver's license the day I turned sixteen, I could never imagine being without a car. In Kansas City, you drove everywhere. I even had a car when I was at college in the dead center of Missouri. And I got here and haven't driven since."

"Yeah, this L.A. boy would be lost without his wheels."

"I don't even want to know how much you pay to park."

"Well, I usually don't drive into work, and besides, I've got a driveway."

"Where do you live, Connecticut?"

"Try again. Brooklyn."

"Huh."

"What's the 'huh' for?" he grinned.

"I just never imagined someone like you living in Brooklyn."

Michael leaned forward to watch for pedestrians before he turned the corner. "Care to explain?"

"You just seem more, I don't know, urban or something."

"And is urban nice-speak for 'uptight?' "

"Okay, so maybe I might have pegged you as a stiff."

Michael covered his heart with a hand. "Ouch, nothing hurts like a zinger from Kate Brown."

And we were off, crossing the Queensboro Bridge with relative ease. And finding a place to park within blocks of the stadium. And shuffling in to Shea Stadium with 50,000 other fans enjoying an afternoon off.

For the first time in God knows how long, I felt relaxed. No tense shoulders, no furrowed brow, no grumbling stomach forming an ulcer. The sun shone on us as we made our way down to the bottom row right at the first-base line.

"How did you score these tickets again, and why aren't they my clients?"

"Actually, they're not from a client. Miranda got them, and she thought that we might like to use them."

" 'We' meaning you and I?"

"Of course. But I have a confession." He cleared his throat. "When Anna heard about the tickets, she told Miranda you were a huge Mets fan, so, here we are."

Good old Anna. And good old Michael for catching on. "Why didn't you take Miranda?"

"Are you kidding? She hates baseball, and besides, she's been so wrapped up with filming that she couldn't get away even if she wanted."

"So you haven't seen much of each other lately?" I inquired casually.

"No, unfortunately. I keep meaning to drop by her set, but that pesky work thing gets in the way."

"Anna seems to be enjoying herself immensely on the set, though we hardly get to talk anymore, now that she's a Hollywood hotshot. I'm so proud of her."

"That's a nice thing to say."

"Well, she *is* my best friend, so I try to throw her a line every now and again." I looked at him. "So tell me a little bit about your best friend. What's his name, does he live in L.A., stuff like that."

Michael sighed. "It's not a he, it's a she. Miranda's my best friend."

I tried to avoid it, but all roads apparently led back to Miranda. And why not? Besides being inhumanly gorgeous, she has charisma, style, smarts, and a sense of humor. And she's so damned nice, plus she gave my best friend the job of her dreams. "Miranda's really great. How did Hollywood not get to her?"

"Family. She's really close to the whole family—aunts, uncles, cousins, you name it. Her dad wouldn't have a prima donna in his household, and she doesn't want one in hers, either."

"Sheesh, is there anything this woman can't do?" Michael opened his mouth to answer, but the Mets took the field, and I leapt from my seat and started shouting. He looked startled.

"FYI," I said between shouts, "I can't be held accountable for anything that escapes my mouth during a Mets game." Michael scanned me quizzically. "I sometimes forget that it's not just me watching the game in front of my TV in the privacy of my own home, so I go a little crazy on the jeers and the slandering."

"Should I be afraid that security might have to escort us out? I don't want to show up on the scoreboard being hauled out of my first New York baseball game."

"It would certainly liven things up, wouldn't it?" The pitcher was setting up for his first throw of the day. "Okay, gotta watch the first pitch." I leaned forward in my seat.

I hooted when he threw a strike, and out of the corner of my eye, I saw Michael flinch. Unexpectedly, I patted his knee. "There, there, don't be afraid."

"It's just interesting how one of the slowest games in the country could make you this hyper."

"Don't worry, they usually get me with the tranquilizer dart by the bottom of the third. And besides, I thought you were a sports fan."

"I am, but I save all my rowdiness for the Lakers."

"Courtside seats?"

"Oh, sure," he casually waved a hand, "me and Jack Nicholson like to talk shop during halftime. No, I usually was in the nosebleed seats, but hey, I was just glad to be there."

"And I'm glad to be here, so thank you." Without barely a breath, I booed with the rest of the crowd when the ump obviously made a bad call and one of the Brewers got a base-on-balls.

I turned to Michael. "I guess I should have warned you that I was über-fan."

He smiled. "No warning necessary. I'm having fun

watching you have fun." I threw my arms up in the air when a double-play ended the first half of the inning.

I turned to him again. "You now have my undivided attention for three minutes."

"Man, you really are rigid when it comes to this game. Have you always been a big baseball fan?"

"Pretty much, but not the Mets until about three years ago. Oh, here's a good story. I went on a date once with a guy when I first moved here who claimed to play for the Kansas City Royals. Little did he know that they were my hometown boys. Totally caught him in a lie. And then you know what he said? 'Did I say Royals? I meant Chiefs. I play football.' At this point I was thoroughly creeped out, but like the naïve 22-year-old I was, I overlooked it, thinking that he probably would redeem himself. And, of course, he didn't. It's amazing the red flags you can look past when you're younger."

"I hear that."

"So, what was your worst date, Michael?"

"You mean I have to pick just one? When I was in my early twenties, I went on a date with an incessant nose-picker."

"Eww!" I cried.

"Wait, I've got one better. Also in my early twenties, I was set up with this girl through one of my friends. Really good looking and smart, he said. And she was. The only trouble was, even though she was 21, she had a strict curfew."

"That's creepy."

"Oh, it gets better. Her dad was two tables away

from us, making sure no one took advantage of his little girl."

"Poor guy. The early twenties just weren't your years for dating."

He shrugged and looked right at me. "Maybe my luck will change."

Suddenly, he shifted uncomfortably. "I, uh, think I'm going to buy a hot dog."

"But the Mets are just getting up to bat!" I cried.

"Don't worry," he assuaged me, "they'll be up again at least another 24 times."

"Well, in that case, bring back two for me." He chuckled and shook his head as he started walking up the cement steps. "I'm serious!" I called after him. "I want everything but onion on them too." He looked scared, which is probably why he obliged.

By the time Michael had returned, an entire inning had passed. I greedily grabbed the hot dogs. "Thank you, thank you, thank you! I was worried you weren't coming back. I wasn't kidding earlier when I said I wanted to eat my weight in hot dogs. You looked a little put off when I put in my request to you for them."

"Not put off, just surprised, once again."

"I suppose where you're from, girls don't eat hot dogs."

"Where I'm from, girls don't eat."

"Too bad. They're missing out!" I took a delicious bite of my hot dog, perfectly dressed up with condiments. I examined it, impressed. "Did you put this dog together?"

Michael nodded proudly. "My first job was at a hot dog stand in Santa Monica when I was fifteen."

"And you're the one who's surprised? Look at you, Mr. Suave Publicist, with meager beginnings at a hot dog cart. It's like an E! True Hollywood Story."

"If nothing else, my dad gave me a strong work ethic. Any job was one worth doing right." He leaned forward and grabbed a bag. "Here, I got you this, too."

"More hot dogs?" I said hopefully, having almost polished off my first one. I reached into the bag and pulled out a starched New York Mets jersey.

"I wanted to give you one of those foam finger thingies, but they were fresh out." He glanced down, looking rather shy.

"Wow. Wow." I shook my head in disbelief. "Get ready to be surprised again, Michael, because I'm speechless."

"I'm glad."

"Glad I'm speechless?"

"No, no, glad you like it. Do you have one?"

"Uh, no. The only thing I have is a faded National League Champions T-shirt from when they played the Yanks in the Subway Series." I slipped the jersey on over my red v-neck shirt. "How much do I owe you?"

"Are you kidding? Nothing. Consider it a one-month anniversary gift."

"A what?"

"Um, uh, one month anniversary of the start of the Devin account," he stammered. "Not our anniversary, no. That would just be, well, odd." I watched Michael stare straight ahead at the pitcher's mound, shoulders slightly slumped.

I didn't get it. We were talking, laughing, having a

great time, and then he made that off-the-cuff comment. What did it mean? Why did I care? I chewed my
nails haphazardly. Needless to say, my enthusiasm for
the game, and for Michael, waned.

## Chapter Ten

"**A**re you interested in him? Even a little bit?" Anna and I walked briskly through Central Park. She was her trendy little self with black yoga pants, a black knit tank top—and the only redhead I know who could pull off a pink bandana.

"No, and you know how I know? I ate two hot dogs in front of him with the works. Did you hear me? Two. And I didn't even flinch. Now, if this were a date, I would have sat politely and pretended that hot dogs made me sick. Besides, he made some off-handed comment that I can't get out of my head."

"Uh, oh. Was it an innocuous comment that you interpreted as hostile?"

"Hostile's not the word. Just perplexing. Things seemed fine. He bought me a jersey and said it was for—"

Anna halted. "Hold up. He bought you a jersey?

That's certainly something above and beyond the call of duty."

"What do you mean?"

Anna shook her head, her foolish apprentice not yet as wise as she. "Michael, who you've only known for what, six, seven months, bought you a jersey of your favorite sports team."

My forehead crinkled as I tried to process what exactly had happened between the two of us the day before at the ballgame. "He was just being nice," I limply suggested.

"Holding doors open is nice. Taking you to a Mets game is nice. Buying you a jersey? I dunno, sounds like someone's got a bit of a crush on you."

"Wait a sec," I raised a hand as we followed a curve on one of the walking trails. "Ain't nobody crushing on no one. Right after he got me the jersey, that's when he got weird." And I told Anna about the anniversary comment.

Anna shook her head. "Poor guy."

"What?" I exclaimed. "He's the one who's the weirdo here, and you're giving him the 'poor guy' treatment?"

"Don't you see? He was nervous. He was probably just trying to cover up his feelings."

"Sure, feelings of regret and remorse for inviting me to the game in the first place."

Anna pointed a stern finger at me. "Uh, uh, uh, none of this negative self-talk. Besides, I'll just get the inside scoop from Miranda," Anna offered casually.

"Please, don't bother."

"You're at least keeping the jersey, right?"

"I may find him somewhat bizarre, but I'm not stupid!"

We picked up our brisk pace again. "Kate, I really don't think Michael is a bad guy. Maybe he's just not good around women. Do you know his dating history?"

"He briefly mentioned an ex-fiancée a while back, and we shared horror dating stories. Oh, and that's another thing. He gave me this weird look and said that maybe his dating luck would change."

"Don't you see? He is interested in you!" I could sense Anna's exasperation with me. "That's it, I'm getting some more details on him from Miranda."

"No!"

"Why so adamant?" Anna raised a suspicious eyebrow.

"Why get her involved? My theory is that those two have something going on on the side, and besides, I need to learn to deal with this Michael thing on my own, since if we nail this Devin thing, we're going to be working together for a long time."

"First of all, I highly doubt those two have anything going on between them. She talks about him like a friend, not someone she's dating. Second of all, quit being so darn stubborn and just accept my help. What harm is there in talking to Miranda?"

"Gee, I don't know, it could make things even more awkward between me and Michael, if that's even possible? Thanks for the offer, hon, but I'll just handle it on my own."

"Not even the slightest bit interested in him?" Anna

squeaked in a small voice, moving together her forefinger and thumb.

"I can't believe we're still talking about this. You're the one who has the big news going on. I feel like we haven't talked in ages, now that you have to report to a movie set every day."

"I am busier than I could have ever imagined."

"Good busy or bad busy?"

"Great busy! I don't get to hang out much on the set, and when I do, it's just for touch-ups, but the eye candy doesn't hurt. Mmm-hmm." Anna licked her lips.

"All right, who is he?"

"Let's just say that a certain Andrew Trotter has requested me as his personal makeup artist."

I gave a blank stare, and Anna laughed. "Holy cow, Kate, you really are clueless! I'm amazed at how you can work in PR and not know who these famous actors are."

"I have never heard of this guy in my life."

"So I might have exaggerated a titch when I called him famous." Anna shrugged. "He was on some daytime soap for a year, and this is his first movie. He's doing a supporting role in the film. I can't believe he didn't get his big break until now. Whew. Is he good looking."

"Perfect. You go to work, you have the promise of hooking up with a hottie. Karma is on your side. I'm happy for you, really, I am. And by the way, can we slow it down a bit? We're practically running. And you know I won't run even if I'm being chased."

"I can't help it! Thinking of Andrew must have just gotten me going. I just have to take care of the Tommy thing."

"You're still stringing him along?" I almost felt bad for the guys Anna dated; I sometimes thought I empathized more with them than with her.

"Oh, he'll be fine. You want to date him?"

"No, thanks, what with the publicity makeover of my ex-boyfriend and fending off affronts from my coworker, I'm plenty occupied. So, when can you take your soul-cleansing trip?"

"That's the problem. No time with this schedule on the set."

"Oh, is that going to be acceptable to break ritual?" I teased.

"Maybe Andrew can be my soul-cleansing trip this time around, if you know what I mean."

"How do you just hop from guy to guy? Teach me, oh wise one."

"I've tried!" Anna was almost indignant. "But you want no part of it. I still think if you and Michael got your feelings out there, things would be much better between you two."

"Oy, why do you keep bringing him up?"

"In all seriousness, I think he might have a thing for you."

"Again, why do you keep bringing him—this—us up?"

"I want what any girl wants for her best friend . . . her happiness."

"Are you going to give me your philosophical speech again about what it means to be happy?"

Anna squinted. "Come on, now, that's not fair."

A twinge of guilt nudged me. "You're right, I might be a little on the testy side lately."

"I can't blame you," Anna replied sympathetically. "You have a lot of pressure going on in your life, what with an ex-boyfriend and a new boyfriend."

"Ack, quit pushing my buttons!"

"But it's so much fun." Anna girlishly skipped. "For real, anything new with Devin? By the way, I can't believe that jerk showed up at the restaurant a few weeks ago."

"Has Miranda said anything about him?"

"Not a word. There doesn't seem to be much connection between the two of them."

"That may be what Miranda thinks, but Devin believes otherwise." I tilted my head. "They haven't been seeing each other, you think?"

"I'm pretty sheltered at work, believe it or not."

"Come on, isn't the makeup artist the one who gets all the dish on movie sets and leaks to the press?"

"Hey, why am I the one being grilled here? He's your client."

"Fortunately, I haven't had to see him the last two weeks. Had some other stuff I had to spin for a CFO at a major company."

"Oh, I love it when you talk work. So cryptic, so vague."

"Only about the confidential stuff. I really could care less about this Devin thing."

Anna stopped dead in her tracks and gave me a knowing look.

I 'fessed up. "Who am I kidding? It's all I can think about, how to get Devin to clean up his act so I can get on with my life. You wanna talk about vague and cryptic? Well, there you go."

"When do you see him next?"

"There's a charity golf tournament this weekend on Long Island."

"It wouldn't be Heart Links, would it?"

"Why yes, it would."

"I think Miranda's going to be on one of the teams. She actually enjoys the charity stuff."

I rolled my eyes. "How convenient. Looks like I'll get to play buffer once again between Miranda and Devin. If he keeps showing up like this, she's going to need a restraining order against him."

Anna smiled. "Not the kind of publicity you're going for, I imagine?"

"Are you sure you don't want to go in my stead?" I pleaded with Anna. "I can pretty much guarantee there will be fireworks."

Apparently I was now the one picking up speed, as Anna had to jog a few paces to keep up with me. "Man, this topic sure got you hot under the collar. Look at you, chastising me earlier for walking too fast."

"I obviously have some steam to burn off."

"At least you're not running away from your problems. You're just walking really fast."

"Har, har. What, exactly, do you think I can do to make this situation better?"

"Hey, you're the doer in this friendship. I make suggestions, you make it happen."

"I'm just tired of my head spinning all the time. Some people thrive on the drama." I looked over at Anna.

She put a hand to her chest. *"Moi?"*

"You know what I mean. You're quite enjoying this Andrew-Tommy situation. If that were me, I would just give up."

"Yes, and why do you give up so easily?" Anna demanded.

I grabbed the towel that had been tucked inside the hip of my red workout pants and dabbed the back of my neck. "I wouldn't say I'm giving up. I just want things to be simple."

"Let's see." Anna stopped and authoritatively put her fist on her hip. "You're a publicist for your ex-boyfriend who keeps trying to paw the most popular actress in Hollywood, all the while trying to deny your feelings for the perfect guy. I'd say you passed simple a long time ago, friend."

## Chapter Eleven

"**J**enna, it's so great to see you." And I wasn't putting on my PR personality; I really was glad to see a friendly face.

"It's been so long. Is Gwen still her neurotic self?" Jenna worked at Burton Relations three years ago and had left for a job offer as a weekend anchor in Buffalo.

"Even more so. Some people slow down with age, but not her. It's not even hyperactivity, really. I can't describe it. I just live it."

"I can't believe you're still working for her." Jenna shook her head, her perfectly coifed blond hair barely moving.

I could only shrug. Why was I still working for Gwen? Sure, I was making decent money and moving up the ranks quite nicely, but was there more than this? Or had I been so tainted by the Devin project that I couldn't tell right from wrong?

"Hello, where did you go?" Jenna teased me, waving her hand in front of my eyes.

"Just got lost in thought. So, what brings you back from Buffalo?"

"Oh, some of the Buffalo Bills are participating in this golf tournament, so I jumped at the chance to come back to the city—well, technically, we're not in the city now, but that's where I'm staying."

"Do you miss it?" I hadn't realized how much a part of the New York fabric I had become; I couldn't imagine going back to a small town.

"I did at first. Ooh, was I miserable. I lived in a pretty quiet—and by that I mean boring—neighborhood, and I thought, 'I left a somewhat decent job in the city I loved for a decent job in a city I can't stand?' But after about six months, I found my niche, and I couldn't imagine leaving. And you'd be surprised by the amount of good-looking men there. And they don't have this pretentious 'I live in the city and am important' thing going on."

"That must be refreshing."

"It is. I come back here and see the lights, the glamour, just the energy, and I really love being in Manhattan. But every time I get back to Buffalo, I'm glad to be home. I never thought I would be that girl."

"Sometimes we're put into situations that we'd never imagined," I said as I looked at Devin, who was chumming it up with the other golfers on his team. He wore a Titleist cap, navy-blue polo shirt, and khakis.

Jenna followed my gaze. "Say, isn't that Devin Underhill? I haven't heard much about him lately."

"Well, you are in Buffalo."

"Hey, I'm still connected!" Jenna joked. "Just because I moved doesn't mean I don't live vicariously through the New York gossip scene. Yeah, for a while there, Devin seemed to be all over the map with the women. But he seems to be getting a grasp on things, or something like that."

I smiled, "I must be doing my job then."

Jenna stepped back. "No way, he's your client?"

"Yep. We're doing some work for him and the Hotel Bella chain. I suppose you wouldn't be interested in doing an interview with him?" It was worth a shot, at least, to get him some upstate publicity.

"I don't know, Kate. I'm not sure it would really resonate with our viewers." She looked more closely at where he was standing. "On the other hand, I do see that he's on a team with one of Bills, so maybe that's my angle. I could never say no to a friend."

"And as your friend, I should warn you that Devin might try to hit on you, so be on guard. Remember, this is your friend speaking, not his PR lackey."

"Thanks for the warning," she smiled. "I think I'll be able to hold my own."

"That's what I thought, but then—"

Jenna tilted her head. "Then what?"

*Woops.* I almost slipped about Devin and I dating. I must not get too lax, even with good friends who happen to be in the media and could make or break his personality makeover. "Oh, I was just going to say that he's a charmer, that's all," I covered.

I walked over to Devin and tapped him on the shoulder. "Sorry to interrupt, but there's an affiliate here from Buffalo who'd like to interview you about your expectations for the tournament today."

He excused himself from the group of men, who were mingling while waiting to golf their next hole. "Buffalo, eh? I've officially made it."

"Don't be a jerk. This is an old friend of mine who happens to be doing a favor for us. And you're playing with one of the Buffalo Bills, so try to act like you know what's going on."

"Lee Evans? Yeah, I know who he is. You're so persnickety."

"You call it persnickety, I call it organized. Thank you for doing this," I said curtly.

We walked over to Jenna and I did the formal introductions. I stood back while Jenna's cameraman made adjustments and she and Devin did some small talk before the interview. It seemed innocuous; maybe Devin could talk to a beautiful woman without clubbing her over the head and dragging her back to his cave.

"Rolling in three, two, one," the cameraman announced.

"Devin, could you tell us a bit about why you're in this tournament to help prevent heart disease?" Jenna asked off-camera.

"I was just talking to Lee Evans about how I had lost my mother to a heart attack, so it was good for me to be out here to help the cause. And, it can't hurt to get a head start on the golf season," he said with a laugh, trying to lighten up the mood from his previous comment.

There was some more idle commentary between the two of them before the camera stopped rolling and they parted ways with a firm handshake. How had I forgotten that his mom, Vivian Underhill, had died of a heart attack ten years ago? It was all over the news, but it was also before my time in New York—and my time with Devin. He never once brought her up, never had any pictures of her on display. I had to believe that what he said to Jenna was more than just a sound bite.

Jenna grabbed my elbow. "Listen, Kate, I have to chase down some other players. It was so good to see you. Thanks for recommending the Devin interview. I was skeptical at first, but that stuff about his mom will really resonate with any audience. And don't worry, he was a perfect gentleman."

"Thank you for agreeing to do the interview," I said blankly, my mind still on Devin. "Take care of yourself."

I started walking toward Devin, who had returned to his teammates. But I immediately stopped, wondering what good it would even do to bring up his mom. It was probably enough for him to have even talked about her, so why salt the wound?

"You look lost in thought." Michael had appeared beside me.

"Nah, I always look like that."

Michael smiled in acknowledgment. "You're right, you kind of do."

"Did you know that Devin's mom died of a heart attack? I can't believe I didn't make the connection to that and this tournament."

"Yeah, last week he said this is the one charity event

he's always certain to do every year. All the other stuff we're asking him to do is just fluff in his mind."

"Well, he gave a great interview to one of the Buffalo stations." Michael opened his mouth to say something, but I put my hand up. "Before you say anything, I think we should try to get a copy and get some of the stations to run it here."

"Can't hurt, I guess."

"So, where did you disappear to?"

"I was watching Miranda golf a few holes. I basically taught her how to play while I was still living in California. So I was just following her around, being half cheerleader, half coach."

I envisioned her learning to golf and flirtatiously saying, "Michael, I just can't just seem to get it right!" And he would walk up behind her, reach around her taut abdomen, and put his hands on top of hers showing her how to swing. Back and forth, back and forth, like a pendulum. Ugh, why did I care?

"Do you golf?" Michael jolted me back to the present.

"Not well, and not often. You know where most of my golf knowledge comes from? That Golden Tee arcade game. How pathetic is that."

Michael blinked. "Not pathetic in the least. You're something else."

"Why, because I'm addicted to arcade games?"

"No, it's just that—"

But he didn't get to finish his thought, as Miranda came bounding toward us. She was wearing braids, a white visor, a white blouse, a pink sweater vest, and white capris. "I got a hole in one on the 18th!" She leapt in pure joy and embraced Michael. She broke away from Michael and then hugged me with the same fervor. "I haven't seen you all day, Kate. How have you been?" She backed away and looked me up and down. "As always, you look so cute!"

I wore baby blue cropped pants with a flair at the bottom, black wedged, open-toe sandals, and a white, long-sleeved blouse with a blue tie around the waist. I'll admit, I bought the outfit for today's tournament. A little retail therapy at H & M last night certainly helped calm the nerves.

"Miranda, have I told you lately how good you are for the ego?"

"She means what she says," Michael directed toward me.

Miranda shot him a look. "Kate, I'm dying of thirst. Want to go back to the clubhouse and get a soft drink?"

"That sounds good. Michael, will you keep an eye out for Devin?"

"Of course. You and Miranda have fun. I might even try to talk to some of these press hounds to get a good shot of Devin on the golf course."

"Thanks. We'll be back soon."

It took Miranda and me twenty minutes for what should have been a two-minute walk, but she had to stop every three feet to sign autographs. And she did it all happily. I couldn't blame Devin and Michael for wanting to be in her presence all the time; it was infectious.

We finally made it to the clubhouse. "I'll take a Coke," Miranda ordered politely from the bar in the dining room. She turned on her stool. "How 'bout you?"

"I'll take a Coke as well."

"That a girl, who needs that diet soda crap."

"There are some things I won't compromise on, and delicious, sugary soda is one."

"Funny, regular soda is something I won't give up, either. You order a Coke in L.A., and they look at you like, 'Did you mean wheat grass instead?' "

"I don't know if I'd make it out there. I barely keep my head above water here."

She looked me in the eye. "Don't be so hard on yourself, Kate."

I blushed, getting self-esteem advice from this goddess who had drawn whispers and admiring stares from others in the restaurant.

She must have sensed my uncomfortability and changed the subject. "So, Michael tells me you went to a Mets game."

"Yes, I forgot to thank you for those tickets. So, thank you so much. I had a great time." For the first two innings, I wanted to add.

"My pleasure. Anna had told me how much you were into the Mets, so it was the least I could do."

"Well, between the tickets and the dinner at Mod, I probably owe you about six months of manual labor."

She waved her hand. "Don't even worry about it. I'm having fun hanging out with you and Anna, who, by the way, is an amazing makeup artist."

"Isn't she? She's doing what she wants. I know she feels forever indebted to you for the opportunity too."

"I'm glad it's worked out for her. And it makes me look good, too, tapping into unused talent."

"Can you get me a job on the set?" I said jokingly.

"Are you serious?" Miranda's eyes flashed.

"Not yet, but I could be. I've been thinking more and more about a change. I'm just starting to run out of steam, especially with this whole Devin thing."

"I'm sorry to hear about the burnout. You should take a vacation. You're welcome to stay at my place in Malibu anytime if you just need a break. You and Michael could come for a visit." She brought a hand to her face. "He's a pretty good guy, huh?"

I was beginning to wonder whether she and Anna were in cahoots. "Yes, I enjoy working with him," I tried to reply without emotion.

"I think his only flaw is that he doesn't always think before he speaks."

"Oh, you've noticed it, too?" We both giggled.

"Take what he says with a grain of salt. He means well, but sometimes he gets ahead of himself and just shoots off at the mouth."

"Hey, pretty lady, I hear you got a hole in one." Devin sauntered toward Miranda. Why did Devin keep appearing at the most inopportune times?

"Another $5,000 to charity for that shot. I'm thinking that my next stop is the Masters." She seemed disinterested but continued to talk to him.

"They could use someone like you," Devin winked.

"How was your score?"

"Let's just say I brought the team average down, or up, however you want to look at it." Miranda looked confused.

"Eight over," he said flirtatiously, then became

solemn. "But it's all for a good cause. My mom died of a heart attack."

Miranda's face fell, and she sympathetically squeezed Devin's wrist.

"It's just so . . . so . . . I mean, family is so important to me." He lowered his head. "And I know it's important to you, too, Miranda."

I leaned forward on my stool and propped my arms on the bar. This I had to hear.

"Well, sure, I, uh—" Miranda stuttered, looking caught off guard.

"I've read a lot of interviews with you where you said family was your number one priority," Devin said mechanically, as if reading from a script. "And it is with me too. My dad and I have never been closer."

I rolled my eyes. What I witnessed in our conference room between Devin and Fox a month ago could not be misconstrued as closeness.

"As you said in *Never Tomorrow*, 'If you don't have family, you don't have love.' And we all need love."

Miranda scratched the back of her neck. "Wow, you've seen that movie? That's, well, surprising, to say the least." She cleared her throat. "Excuse me, but I need to make a run to the ladies' room."

Devin pounded his fist on the bar, and I moved into Miranda's seat. "What," I exclaimed, "were you doing there?"

"Getting to know a new friend."

"She didn't seem all that interested."

He shrugged. "Give it time."

"And what was all that stuff about family?"

"Hey, can you fault me for doing my research?" Devin smirked. "She's kind of a tough nut to crack, so I thought this would soften her up a bit, you know, get her talking about family."

And then it hit me. "Oh, don't even tell me. You're using your dead mom as leverage with Miranda!"

"Shh, don't say it like that. Then I'll never get her where I want her."

Could this man have been even more soulless than what I had originally thought? I swung around on my chair, only to find Michael standing right behind us. "Get her where you want her, huh?"

When he should have looked ashamed, Devin was confidently grinning. "Hey, man, you know what it's like."

Michael raised his chest. "No, actually, I don't."

I felt the electricity jumping between the two men. No need to have the press picking up on a fistfight between a publicist and his client.

I stood up. "Listen, I think we should all go our separate ways." Devin and Michael just stared at each other.

Then Miranda walked up. "What's going on?"

I pulled her aside. "I think we should go."

"That was my plan anyway," she whispered confidentially. "I was getting a really weird vibe off of Devin."

I walked up to Devin. "Well, thanks for participating in the event today," I said dryly. "Miranda has somewhere else she needs to be, and so do Michael and I."

Devin tried to stand tall and proud, but I saw his nostrils give a slight flare.

"Can I offer you a ride anywhere?" he asked Miranda, almost desperately.

She flashed him a sympathetic smile. "No, I'm in good hands, thanks."

Miranda and Michael walked out of the clubhouse. I followed, but Devin yelled after me.

"Kate!"

I turned to look, naively thinking that he might apologize for his behavior.

"Wanna come back to my place?"

I searched his face for signs of remorse, embarrassment, sincerity—anything that would assure me that he was, in fact, human. But I found nothing, so I walked out the door.

## Chapter Twelve

"**I** kind of feel bad for him," Miranda said softly.

"That man deserves nothing, especially not your sympathy." Michael's eyes narrowed emphatically as Miranda's limo drove us back to the city. This was the most emotional I had ever seen him.

Miranda checked her pink watch, which had diamonds surrounding the face. "Do you guys mind if I have the driver drop me off at my hotel, then take you back to your houses? I need some time to unwind before this party I have tonight."

"Not at all," I replied. I, too, was looking for some time to unwind, and that's all I had planned for the rest of the weekend.

After we pulled up to the Waldorf Astoria, Miranda's driver had opened the door for her. She leaned over and gave us each a hug. "Thanks, you two, for your help

124

with the Devin situation today. Michael, I'll call you tomorrow. Kate, we need to go out, just us girls."

I stared out the window absently as we pulled away. "Shouldn't we be worried that Devin's going to take off and undo all the good PR we've been giving him?"

Michael snickered. "I think his plans for the evening went awry."

"That's exactly my fear. Because he had intentions to keep Miranda all to himself this weekend, and that fell through, he will go out trolling for someone else."

"Has anyone told you that you worry too much?"

I ignored him. "All I can imagine is something showing up in next week's papers, and Gwen will have our heads."

"It'll be fine."

"Do you really believe that, witnessing what you did just an hour ago?"

"Yes, I do believe it. And even if he does go out, we got him interviewing with your friend, saying some powerful stuff about his mom and the charity tournament today."

"If only others buy it, since apparently Devin didn't."

Michael sighed as he looked at me. "I wanted to believe Devin, really, I did, but what I overheard him say in the clubhouse about Miranda . . ." His words trailed off. "I mean, who says that? I don't know, Kate, we just need to be done on this project. I'm really starting to dislike the guy."

I nodded empathetically, bemused that Devin had gotten under Michael's skin like this.

The limo driver turned to look over his shoulder at us. "West 126th Street, right?"

"Yup, that's right." I faced Michael. "By the way, is your car still on Long Island?"

"Nope, it's in Brooklyn. Miranda's driver picked me up. I've been in a limo more today than I have in the past three years."

"I don't do well in limos. For whatever reason, I always feel guilty, or like a poser."

"A poser? Wow, there's a flashback to junior high."

"Oh, didn't they use words like that in California?" I gently nudged him.

"Nah, but I heard it on TV once."

"Two more blocks, second building on the right," I directed the driver.

Michael rubbed his sideburn. "So, what are your plans for the evening?" His words sounded a bit forced, almost nervous.

"I just want to sit at home and veg out in front of the TV. I have been going nonstop the last month and just want to relax."

"Isn't that a cardinal sin, a single New Yorker staying home by herself on a Saturday night?"

"Wouldn't be the first time."

"Same here. Honestly, since being on this Devin account, this is the most I've been on the scene since I moved here."

Maybe it was watching him looking out for Miranda, or the overall mood of the day, but I found myself giving Michael a courtesy invite. "Want to order Chinese and stare at the idiot box with me?"

"That sounds like a lot of fun, as long as I'm not intruding."

Hmm. That was a surprise. His answer was supposed to sound something like, "Geez, Kate, I would love to, but I have a lot to get done around the house tonight."

Instead, all I could say was, "No, you're not intruding at all."

We walked up the two flights of stairs to get to my apartment. It was odd to think that a little over a month ago, we had been in this exact place, mulling over how to help Devin's image. But now, it was a Saturday evening, and we were off the clock, I became very aware.

I threw my keys on a plant stand by my front door and bolted it once Michael had entered after me. I walked to the kitchen and opened my junk drawer, which was filled with old bills, a pair of scissors, and most importantly, takeout menus. I grabbed a few and brought them out to Michael, who had taken a seat on my purple couch.

"My recommendation is Wang's Chinese, but any of those are good."

"I'll take whatever you recommend. What from Wang's do you usually get?"

"Sesame chicken, medium spice. Pretty uninventive."

"Ever tried the chicken and cashews?"

I leaned over his shoulder to read the menu description and caught a whiff of the cologne I had smelled outside the restaurant. "Nope." I hope he didn't notice the pause. "It has mushrooms, and I'm allergic to those."

"That's too bad. How did you find that out?"

"I think it was an adult-onset thing. Anna and I had

taken a trip to Seattle our senior year of college for spring break, and the night before we were heading back home, we had a nice dinner. I had never liked mushrooms, but I'd eat them occasionally. And I didn't ask if my dish had mushrooms in it, but I ate it anyway. In the middle of the night, I woke up with horrible nausea and, well, I barely made it to the bathroom. Not because I wasn't fast enough, mind you, but because my eyes were swollen shut."

Michael wrinkled his nose. "You didn't fly home, did you?"

"I had no choice. We were poor college students and couldn't afford to pay for another night in Seattle, so I slept in the back of the plane on the floor, right by the bathroom. The flight attendants were great about it. I sent the airline a letter of apology about being so sick, I felt so guilty."

"They were probably happy to get a letter of apology rather than having to write one." He shook his head. "Some spring break. Why Seattle, by the way?"

"I'm not the Daytona Beach/Cancun/South Padre type—at least I wasn't at the time. I was an angst-ridden college student. 'Oh, those places are so cliché,' Anna and I would haughtily say. But now, those places are rather intriguing to me. Sort of a regressive thing, one might say." I pointed over Michael's shoulder at the menu. "So, what can I order for you?"

"If I get the cashew chicken, will you get sick?"

"Nah, maybe just gag." I teased. "I can be near them, just can't eat them. You mean I didn't gross you out with my mushroom story?"

"I'm so hungry, nothing can affect this appetite. So that's what I'll have." He reached into his wallet and pulled out a twenty.

"Put that away," I ordered. "I already owe you at least twice that for the dinner that one night." And the cab fares. And the hot dogs. And the baseball jersey. Suddenly guilt settled over me, along with the wonder of how Michael had so much disposable cash.

After placing our order, I ran to the refrigerator to see what our beverage choices were. A Brita pitcher full of water and a two-liter of Sunkist were all I had. Had I really been so wrapped up with work that I couldn't even stock my refrigerator?

I gave the choices to Michael.

"Sunkist?" he laughed.

"I have no idea why I have that. I haven't had it since third grade."

"I'll take it. Orange sugar water sounds oddly refreshing right now."

"How about I serve it in wine glasses, and that'll make us feel like grown-ups?" I smiled.

Michael broadly grinned in return. It was nice to see him smile, considering how intense he always seemed.

With two Sunkist-filled wine glasses, I came back to the living room, where Michael had been looking through the few DVDs I owned.

He jumped back like a little kid caught in the cookie jar. "Sorry," he lamely apologized. "I guess I didn't notice your movies the last time I was over here. I'm surprised that most of these are romantic comedies."

"I'm surprised you know what a romantic comedy is."

"Well, I would have called them 'chick flicks,' but you'd probably have kicked me out by now." He had put the five DVDs back in their place. "You don't have anything with Miranda!" he said in mock horror.

"Shh, don't tell her. I'll go out and buy one of her movies tomorrow, I swear."

Michael sipped the orange soda. "You know, I would've never pegged you as the romantic comedy type."

I raised an eyebrow. "Really? What type of movies do you think I should own?"

"Anything that premiered at Sundance."

"Thanks, I guess. So, what's in your collection?"

"A lot of war movies."

I wrinkled my nose.

"Hey, have you ever seen a war movie? They're not all that bad."

"Did you ever have to do spin for your clients in Hollywood if they ever did bad movies?"

"Yeah, one time I spent an hour on the phone with an editor at *Entertainment Weekly* trying to persuade him that Courtney Love and Ben Affleck really did make a believable match on-screen."

A-ha! The rumor was true. "So, you worked for Courtney Love?" I tried to act casually.

"For like a week." Michael shook his head and laughed, his eyes brightening. "Then I handed her over to a fellow publicist, who thrived off the commotion that followed her everywhere. And that was right around the time things were going sour between me and

Jillian, so I just wasn't needing the drama." He became serious at the mention of the ex-fiancée, but gave a quick chuckle. "Then again, Devin ranks right up there on the drama scale. It certainly has introduced me to the city, that's for sure."

I tilted my head. "What do you mean?"

"As weird as it sounds, this Devin thing is the most social I've been since I've moved here."

I felt a tinge of sympathy for Michael. "What do you usually do for fun?"

"I go out exploring by myself. I go to the gym, because no matter how far I get away from L.A., I will always be a gym rat." I unexpectedly found myself trying to casually look at his pecs through his white polo shirt, tucked into his khaki pants. I was pretty sure he was ripped, but I stared a few seconds longer just to make sure. Yup, it was confirmed.

"How 'bout you? What do you do for fun?" He raised an eyebrow, noticing that I was staring at his chest.

"Oh, you mean other than giving a personality make-over to my ex-boyfriend?" I hastily covered. "I hang out with Anna a lot. I have some other friends I do dinner with once every few months, but Anna and I are like sisters—or at least what I imagine a sister should be like. Wouldn't know, since I was an only child, and an 'oops' at that."

"Well, I have a sister, and although the brother-sister relationship is different than the sister-sister relationship, we still get along pretty well." He crossed his legs out in front of him and stretched his arms above his head. "Of course, we still get under each other's skin from time to time, but we respect each other, and that's a great quality to have."

"You mean you don't get into knock-down, drag-you-by-the-hair fights at this age?" I smirked.

"My sister . . ." Michael hesitated.

"Yes?" I encouraged.

"She's someone you—" We were interrupted by a knock at the door. I leapt off the purple couch where I had been sitting facing Michael, to get to the door. I returned immediately with our food, packaged in one large brown bag.

"This is why I love Wang's—they're cheap, they're fast, and they love me for ordering from them at least once a week." I started taking the food out of the bag and setting it on the pine coffee table with dark-brown varnish. "Anyway, what were you saying about your sister?"

"It's not important," Michael said dismissively. "I can't wait to eat. I don't think I've ever been this hungry."

"I hear that. Let me get some silverware before you have to resort to turning it into finger food."

As I gathered plates and forks from my kitchen, I thought about how it was eating out with Devin. I'm up for trying new foods, but with him, it was always the highest-priced restaurants, always ordering food I couldn't pronounce, let alone recognize, always pretending that I really liked *foie gras* when all I wanted was a cheeseburger. It was nice that Michael didn't have any of those pretenses and was just willing to dive into some good old-fashioned comfort food. Devin wouldn't have been caught dead ordering from a place like Wang's.

Wait, was I just comparing Devin to Michael? And Michael came out ahead? Now, now, I mustn't be thinking like that, I thought, but there was that muffled voice in the back of my head that squeaked, "Why not?"

After a deep breath to compose myself, I came back to the living room and set the dishes on the table. Michael reached for them as I was moving my hand away. We brushed fingers, every so slightly, and the back of my neck tingled. He cleared his throat, and I wiped my hands on my pants.

I sat down and concentrated on biting, chewing, swallowing, anything but Michael. But that voice I heard in the kitchen got a little bit louder. "Why not?"

## Chapter Thirteen

"She's alive!" Michael said in his best Vincent Price voice.

I slowly looked up from my desk to see Michael in my doorway. "Well, happy Monday to you, too."

"I didn't think you were going to get up until Tuesday the way you went out Saturday night."

Rita, the administrative assistant, happened to be walking by at that moment, and she raised an eyebrow. I shot her an "it's not what you think" look, but she smirked and continued walking.

I looked at Michael, vaguely recalling Saturday night. "Pardon?"

"We ate our takeout, you popped in a movie, and you passed out."

Yes, it was coming back to me. I remember looking at the clock on the DVD player at 12:32, and it was dark outside. I had no recollection of whether Michael was still there. When I woke up for good at 4 P.M. Sunday, I knew that Michael had left. I watched TV for a few hours, absently ate a bowl of dry shredded wheat, and went back to bed, too exhausted to even wonder what happened to Michael.

"So," he said as he looked at his shoes, "you didn't get my note?"

"Note?"

"Oh." He seemed embarrassed. "It's nothing, really. Just didn't want to wake you so I thought I'd leave a note."

"That was sweet," I said softly. "Thanks."

He waved a hand like he was shooing away a fly. "Ah, don't worry about it. Anyway," he quickly switched to business persona, "we didn't even get a chance to talk about the Symphony Ball Thursday night."

"What?" I panicked as I shuffled through my calendar. "I had it down as next Thursday."

"Nope, it's this Thursday."

Frustrated, I put my head in my hands. "I can't even keep my schedule straight!" I took a deep breath. "All right, sorry you had to witness that freak-out. Tell me what needs to be done."

"I called all the papers and TV stations this morning to give them a heads up that Fox Underhill will be there as the guest of honor, considering his $1 million contribution last year to the symphony, and Devin will be going as his guest."

Good old Michael. Smooth, controlled, on top of the game.

As if on cue, Gwen bounded into my office. "Oh, just the pair I was looking for!" Her gaudy silver-and-turquoise earrings swung fiercely. "Say, I need you two to do a favor for that little do-wop on Thursday. You need to go out and buy Devin a new suit."

"Excuse me?" I asked disbelievingly, while Michael grimaced.

"You heard me," she snorted. "Specifically, you need to get it from Hugo Boss. I just got off the phone with their marketing VP, and if we can get Devin in one of their suits and get him some press while he's wearing it . . ." Gwen paused for dramatic effect. "Well, then we'll be doing some business with Hugo Boss, that's all I can say. Anyway, Angie's your contact at the store on 5th Avenue. She's expecting you today. Toodles!" She spun out of my office in her Aztec-printed skirt.

I waited till Gwen was out of earshot. "There have been times when I just wanted to up and quit Burton Relations." I white-knuckled the edge of my desk. "This has to rank in the top five. I mean, what are we, personal assistants? We have to go shopping for a suit now for that weasel?"

"Come on, Kate." Michael was grinning from ear to ear.

"What are you smiling at?" I asked skeptically, yet his smile was contagious; I started giggling.

"See? You have to laugh at it, otherwise stuff like this will drive you nuts. We'll make a day of it. We'll have lunch, get the suit, have a snack, check on the suit, get coffee, talk about the suit, get another snack, and then call it a day."

I nodded. "I like your thinking."

He checked his watch. "Onward and upward. Leave at high noon?"

The morning flew by with the usual tasks of taking and making phone calls, e-mailing, opening mail, filing, surfing the Internet for any mentions of clients. I found an interesting site and shared it with Michael as we walked to Hugo Boss.

"Do you know that some girl in Albany has a Web page devoted to Devin?"

Michael snapped his head toward me. "You've got to be kidding me."

"Her name is Hilary, and she has all these pictures posted of Devin. All the good, wholesome ones, of course. For her sake, I hope she didn't see any of those skanky ones we saw doing our research."

"Wow, Devin has made it. A fan page. Unreal. What does the girl say about Devin?"

"Oh, she pretty much just has a bunch of captions next to his pictures, talking about he is the hottest guy in the whole wide universe and how she is trying to get her parents to swing for a room at Hotel Bella on her 13th birthday." I raised a finger. "And the best part is she talks about how he's really into charity and stuff, to paraphrase, of course."

Michael held open the door for me when we arrived at the grand store with the bright atrium. "If a 13-year-old is seeing our work coming into play, you'd think the rest of New York would catch on soon."

My eyes wandered over the elaborate suits, made of the finest fabrics shipped from halfway across the world. There was a menagerie of charcoals, grays, navys, and even some brighter blues. I felt horribly underdressed in the store, with my beige linen pants and light purple blouse. The store was buzzing with lunchtime traffic, yet a blond clerk immediately found our way to us.

"Can I help you?" she chirped.

"We're looking for Angie," Michael said authoritatively.

"That's me." Suddenly her voice dropped to its normal octave, and she sounded about ten years older. "How can I help you two today?"

"We're from Burton Relations," I offered.

She gave a knowing nod. "Of course," she whispered conspiratorially. "Devin Underhill. Are you his personal assistant?" Angie looked me up and down.

I frowned. "You could say that."

"She's from Burton Relations, too," Michael said, trying to sound as unpatronizing as possible. "So, Angie, what do we need to do?"

"First, you need to choose a suit." Her long, straight blond locks swayed back and forth.

Michael cleared his throat. "I was under the impression that the suit would be ready, and we'd just have to pick it up."

"Well, my impression was that you'd be finding a suit—with my recommendation, of course," she beamed.

Michael pulled me aside and spoke under his breath. "I don't have a good feeling about this. I don't want to be here for two hours trying to find a suit for Devin."

I laughed and gently poked his rib. "Do we have a

choice? And by the way, what happened to 'We have to laugh about these situations?' "

Michael also laughed. "Hey, don't use my words against me!"

"Are we ready?" Angie sang behind us.

We turned to face her. "Sure," I resigned. "What's the first step?"

"Well, do you have Devin's measurements?"

Now how were we supposed to get those? They had to be on file somewhere, maybe where he buys his suits. "I'll get those later," I dismissed. "For now, can we see your suggestions?"

"I have about ten suits in mind." Michael rolled his eyes, but I didn't blink. Angie looked at Michael. "Would you be willing to model for us?"

"Be a good sport," I winked.

He shook his head and sighed. "Who's the one who should be looking for a new job?"

I playfully patted his shoulder. "You'll be fine. Now, get to the dressing room, you."

He stuck out his lower lip and shuffled his feet. Angie shoved a suit toward him, and he reappeared within two minutes.

Angie and I looked at each other with wide eyes, then stared at Michael. He had kept his white button-down shirt on, but the smooth, slate-gray jacket perfectly hugged his broad shoulders, and the matching pants fit him perfectly, especially when he turned around to model his backside.

"I never realized how tall you were" was all I could manage.

He was clueless to our gawking. "Yeah, I'm six-two. How tall did you think I was?"

I pursed my lips. Why hadn't I noticed his height before? And that body? Why did he look like a brand new person in that overpriced suit? All right, girl, slow down, I silently coaxed myself.

"I think you should buy it," I blurted.

Michael squinted. "Kate, you realize how much this costs, right?"

I turned hopefully to Angie. "He could get a discount, right?"

"Forty percent."

"Nah," he shrugged.

"Fifty!" Angie, apparently overcome by her attraction for Michael, was in the mood for bargaining.

"He'll take it," I answered for him. "Look, you, a suit like that for half the price is a steal."

Michael looked at the tag. "I wouldn't say $4,000 is a steal."

"Look at it as an investment," I persuaded.

"If you think it's a good purchase, then I trust your judgment."

Angie cleared her throat, reminding us of her presence. "What about Devin's suit?"

"Oh, right, that's why we're here." I tucked my hair behind my ear. "Angie, we're kind of in a hurry. Why don't you pick out the suit you think is best? I'll fax over his measurements as soon as I get them, and you can send the tailored suit to this address." I wrote down the Hotel Bella corporate office while Michael changed back into his clothes.

"Are you sure?" Angie said softly.

I leaned in closely to her and kept my voice low. "You saw Michael in the first suit he tried on, right? And you saw how good he looked. You picked that out. If you can do wonders with him, think of what you can do for Devin Underhill."

"Just one question," Angie inquired. "Does he have a girlfriend?"

"No, but he's a very busy man, managing all those hotels." I hope I let her down all right.

She blushed. "I was talking about him." She pointed to the changing room.

"Um, well, you know, I don't think—no, he's single." Why was I stumbling over my words? I had no claim to Michael, and he could date whomever he chose. "You should give him your number," I forced myself to say.

She flashed me a grin. "Thanks. I actually thought you two were a couple when you came in here."

I vehemently shook my head. "No, no, no," I said perhaps a little too eagerly. "We're just coworkers. And speaking of coworkers," I raised my voice as Michael walked toward us.

"I'm going to wait outside while you two finish up the order." Angie gave me a knowing grin, excited that I was leaving her alone to make a play for Michael. So why was my stomach turning at the thought of it while I paced on the sidewalk?

Within two minutes, Michael had exited the store. "Hey, why did you leave me all alone in there?"

"Uh-oh, I made you fend off a girl all by yourself," I tried to tease, but it sounded somewhat jaded.

"She tried to give me her phone number, but I just didn't want it."

"What did you tell her?" I was dying of curiosity.

"That I was interested in someone else." He looked at me pointedly, and I felt static travel through my entire body. And then, rather hastily, he said, "That wasn't too bad of a rejection line, was it?"

In one instant, my chest caved in disappointment. How juvenile of me to think that he was talking about me and instead, he was just trying to let Angie down gently. I raised my shoulders and looked straight ahead. There was no reason to be like this, I told myself. We are just coworkers. And I certainly couldn't let myself fall for a coworker, could I?

The night of the Symphony Ball hadn't started out the best for me. The dry cleaners had put my black satin gown on a back shelf, so I maniacally ran to Nordstrom and had to charge $400 to my credit card for a dress that I wasn't all that crazy about. I wore a periwinkle floor-length dress with spaghetti straps, looking more like a bridesmaid throw-away than a publicist trying to look as elegant as possible for one of the most posh fund-raisers in New York City.

As I rushed around my apartment gathering my makeup to put on in the waiting cab downstairs, I saw a piece of paper sticking out from underneath the couch. "Hey, Sleeping Beauty. Didn't want to wake you. See you Monday. Michael."

I thought about that note while I rode in the cab. What a nice gesture. Maybe this was someone I could really like, but then I remembered what he said outside the Hugo Boss store after the Angie incident.

Despite my best efforts, I was still thirty minutes late in meeting Michael at the Ritz Carlton. He paced outside the front entrance, looking panicked and incredibly handsome in his Hugo Boss suit. I expected him to be annoyed with my tardiness, but the first thing he said to me was, "I was worried about you."

I explained everything that had happened. "Well, you can't tell you rushed yourself," he said with a cautious look from my toes to my face. "You look nice. Really nice."

He gave me an intense look, but all I could do was plaster a smile, then hustle into the main ballroom where the event was taking place. The 500-some guests were still mingling, sipping cocktails, waiting for the formal program to start. I spotted Fox right away.

"Kate, what a pleasure to see you." He kissed my left cheek, then lowered his voice. "We haven't had a chance to talk, but you've been doing a fantastic job with Devin. I'm really pleased."

I graciously nodded. "I'm glad to hear it." I was about to subtly ask him whether he felt the project was close to completion; but one of the event committee members tapped him on the shoulder and told him they were about to begin.

"We'll talk more later," he said over his shoulder.

Michael took his place beside me. "What did Fox have to say?"

"He's really happy with what we've been doing for Devin," I smiled broadly.

"Did he say—"

"Whether we were done?" I finished. "No, and I didn't have a chance to ask him."

A sea of glitter, sequins, and black tuxes rushed past us to take their seats. Devin was already seated at one of the front tables with a group of middle-aged women, drumming his fingers on the white tablecloth. But he perked up when his father was introduced as the keynote speaker and led the crowd in a standing ovation.

"Good," Michael nodded as he watched Devin. "That's good."

"You can tell he's miserable," I added, "but at least he's catching on that he should go through the motions."

Fox talked of the importance of giving to charity, while Michael and I notified the reporters and photographers of upcoming photo ops with father and son. Most of them rolled their eyes at us, the pushy publicists, while others obliged and started snapping shots.

After Fox's speech, which garnered him two more standing ovations, the formal dinner of roasted duck and artichoke risotto was served. Michael and I still stood in the back of the ballroom, nibbling on prosciutto tea sandwiches and some other fancy hors d'oeuvres I didn't recognize.

I turned to Michael. "You know what the unfortunate thing about attending these sophisticated events is?"

"You realize how poor you are?" Michael raised an eyebrow.

"Besides that." I smoothed a hand over my left hip. "You never get to enjoy the actual sit-down dinner or the dancing or any of the other fun stuff because you're so busy keeping an eye on your client or making sure the media's doing what you'd like them to do."

The full orchestra, which had been providing quiet dinner music, turned up the volume to indicate that the dancing would begin. Devin and Fox walked to the pristine dance floor with the event co-chairs in hand to do the honorary first dance. The two socialites in their forties both beamed into the eyes of their partners, basking in the charms of the Underhill father-and-son duo. Cameras flashed all around, and I smiled triumphantly. Fox and Devin put on their best face for the evening; there was no sign of the tension I had witnessed in the Burton offices a few months ago. But they were professionals.

More and more couples joined the foursome on the dance floor. I looked around and saw that I was the only one left standing. Where was Michael? At least I would've had someone to talk to. Suddenly I felt like I was in junior high, watching all the popular kids slow dancing. But rather than get sucked into a pity party for one, I welcomed the opportunity to sit down and give my feet, squeezed into open-toed, ivory-colored heels, a much-needed break.

Michael reappeared and hovered over me. "Sorry about that. I saw someone I knew from my days in L.A." He then extended his hand. "For those of us who never get to have any fun . . . may I have this dance?"

"Don't worry," he laughed in response to my frantically looking around the room. "Everyone will be fine for a few minutes. It's just a dance."

He escorted me onto the dance floor, not letting go

of my hand once. I put my left hand on the back of his shoulder, and he gently put his right hand on my waist. I thought I was going to melt. It was the closest physically I had been to a guy in years, and it was Michael, no less. I secretly inhaled his scent of airy cologne and soap and shuddered with pleasure. *Don't do this to yourself, Kate.* I willed myself to withdraw from his grasp, but instead, he drew me closer. Our faces touched as we started swaying in time with the music.

*"How can I tell you what is in my heart? How can I measure each and every part?"* crooned the lead singer with her throaty, soulful voice.

"This is a beautiful song," I whispered in Michael's ear. "I've never heard it."

"It's *How Deep is the Ocean.*" Michael's low voice resonated in my ear.

I watched the singer as I rested my chin on Michael's shoulder. She thoughtfully closed her eyes; it was only she and the music in the room, just as it was only Michael and I in the room. *"How much do I love you? I'll tell you no lie. How deep is the ocean? How high is the sky?"*

Michael gently pulled away from me, his hazel eyes softening. "Kate, I need to talk to you about something."

I looked up at him, expectant, breathless.

"I don't think we should work together any more."

## Chapter Fourteen

"**C**ome see me immediately!"

The note, sticking on my computer monitor, was written in Gwen's frenetic hand. I had been holed up in the conference room all day, and these were my priorities: check my e-mail and voice mail, leave work on time on a Friday for once, and go immediately to a warm bath—with the hopes that it would make me forget about last night.

Last night. It kept rearing its ugly head all day. *"I don't think we should work together any more."* Any rational person would have asked, "Why not?" But I was caught off guard, and I fled the scene. I locked myself in one of the bathrooms at the Ritz, staring at the back of the door. After what felt like an hour, the restroom attendant tapped on the stall.

"Are you okay?" she asked in accented English.

I opened the door and peeked out. "I'll be fine. Just feeling a little dizzy."

The dark-haired woman nodded her head and went back to her post, and I meandered over to the sink and splashed my face. I took a deep breath, mustering any ounce of pride I could find before returning to the dance floor, where Michael was still standing, just as I had left him.

I jutted out my chin. "I think you have all this under control. I'm going home."

"Maybe we could talk about what just happened?" he suggested weakly.

I put my hands on my hips and looked down. "No, I'd rather not," which was a bold lie, because it's all I wanted to talk about, but I didn't want the pain I was feeling to cut any deeper.

So not only did I have the somewhat embarrassing memory of last night, but now I had this note from Gwen to contend with. I rolled my eyes as I grabbed it, crumpled it up, and threw it in the recycling bin. I pushed off from my desk and walked to her office.

"Shut the door."

My heart leapt as I processed the reality of the situation. I had heard the tone and witnessed the start of this routine before, and it usually ended in an employee leaving in tears and packing up her desk.

"What the hell is this?" Gwen shoved toward me a magazine page, the page that happened to feature the one public photo taken of Devin and me.

This was it. The moment I feared from day one of this project. I should have been honest. I should have been up-front. Instead I participated in this charade of pretending I'd never heard of Devin Underhill before and would likely lose my job because of it.

Instead of taking accountability or apologizing for my actions, all I could muster was, "Where did you get that?"

"It doesn't matter."

My eyes clouded. "Did someone hand it to you?"

"If you must know, it was mailed to me. Anonymously." Her eyes bore into me.

Why did I feel like I was part of some covert CIA operation, or a conspiracy and someone was out to get me? "Was there a note attached?"

"No need. The picture explains itself."

"You realize it's from over two years ago, right?"

"You realize you lied to me, right?"

I shifted my eyes toward the ceiling, hoping the tears would retreat. I took a deep breath and returned to steady eye contact with Gwen. "I am really sorry. I guess I got caught up in the idea of a promotion to partner. I'm not making excuses . . ." my words trailed off.

"You know how I feel about liars, Brown."

I bit my lower lip and nodded slightly.

"You're not gonna cry on me now, are you?"

Two tears worked their way down my cheeks. "I'm sorry I disappointed you."

"I'm sorry you did, too, but I know that you're more disappointed in yourself than anyone." It was the softest I had ever seen or heard Gwen. But it was a brief lapse. "Now if you mess this up, there'll be hell to pay."

"Of course, of course. You have my word."

"You're dismissed."

I smoothed my black trousers and rose from the chair, showing myself the door.

I immediately locked myself in my office. I was fortunate to even have an office, though Gwen was *this-close* from taking it away from me. I had dug a grave for myself, and I understood how quickly—and unexpectedly—the career rug could be yanked from underneath you.

There was a brisk knock at my door. It was probably Gwen, here to inform me that she forgot to fire me before I left her office.

"Go away!" I wanted to yell like an angry teenager. But I took a deep breath, blotted my eyes with a tissue, and opened the door. There stood Michael, looking down at a folder in his hands. "Kate, I'm wondering if you could take a look at these press releases for me."

"Sure," I said softly, grabbing the folder and trying to quickly turn so he didn't have to see my puffy eyes. But I wasn't fast enough.

"What's wrong?"

"Just got some bad news, that's all." Don't cry. Don't cry. Don't cry. Thankfully, my weepy ways kept their distance—at least for now.

"Anything I can help with?" Michael's forehead creased; he looked genuinely concerned. "You wanna go out for coffee? Besides, I feel like I should explain my motives for last night. I stopped by your office about ten times today, but you were never there."

"You know me, always busy," I managed weakly, avoiding any significant eye contact.

"I just need to return a quick phone call, and we can run over to Billy's a few blocks from here." He slowly backed out of the office, never taking his eyes off of me.

Regardless of the companion, I was glad to be out of the office. It was one of those magical spring days, the kind that have been romanticized in movies and novels for generations. Wispy clouds scattered themselves overhead in the bright blue sky. The early evening sun was just warm enough to hint at what lay ahead for the rest of the summer.

Michael and I walked to the coffee shop in silence. I was not in the mood for idle talk, and either he sensed that or he, too, had nothing to say. In fact, I preferred the sound of the New York work force all leaving at the same time, as if a school bell had sounded, to soak up the warm sun and start their weekends. It kept my mind, albeit briefly, off my conversation with Gwen today, and my talk with Michael last night.

Michael held open the door for me at Billy's Hut, a coffee shop off the beaten path that probably wouldn't be so cozy once one of the city magazines deemed it "Most Charming Place for a Cup of Coffee" and every other person made it the new place to be seen. I was just glad to know about it before everyone else did, for once. This place comforted me. Billy was a real guy whose family photos hung on the wall. And they weren't the vintage 1890s photos that had become so chic to display. They were taken in the 1970s and '80s, with kids in plaid pants mugging for the camera, or posing on their banana-seat bikes with the ribbon tassels coming out of the handlebars.

Kids who were now my age. Wearing clothes I would have worn. With parents wearing clothes my parents would have worn.

It made me want to cry again.

Michael must have seen my reaction. "Hey, are you going to be all right?"

"Just one of those weeks."

His brow wrinkled. "Let's talk about it."

"Not till I get some caffeine," I said with a half-smile.

"No arguments here. What sounds good to you?"

"Double espresso."

He returned in five minutes with our drinks. We awkwardly sat in silence, me tracing the rim of my coffee mug, him blowing into his latte.

"So, uh," Michael started, "we should talk about last night. I really want you to know that—"

"I'm afraid I might lose my job," I blurted, feeling oddly more comfortable talking about that than last night.

"What?" Michael was incredulous. "Why would you say that? You are Gwen's right-hand woman."

"Yeah, apparently I crossed my mentor today."

Michael raised a confused eyebrow.

"She found out about Devin. That we had a past."

"How?"

"You know that picture you saw of him and me, the one in my apartment? It was mailed to her anonymously." I searched Michael's face for a reaction, and he appeared upset.

"Creep," he mumbled under his breath.

"Who?"

"Come on, this has Devin written all over it."

"Why would he do something like that? It's just a waste of his time."

"All right, if you think it wasn't him, then who could have done it?"

"Miranda?" I knew how stupid it sounded before it even left my mouth, yet I said it anyway. And I hit a nerve, evidenced by the pained expression on Michael's face. "I'm sorry, I don't know why I said that," I recanted. "I'm just upset. Heck, looking at the pictures on the wall in here almost made me sob."

Michael shifted uncomfortably in his chair.

"Don't worry, I won't cry," I assuaged him. "I was just a little jolted after talking with Gwen, that's all. I don't even know where to go from here."

"How did you leave things with her?"

"She basically told me not to screw this up or else."

"Hmm." Michael sipped his coffee thoughtfully. "I only suggest this if you're comfortable with it, but what if I talked to Gwen about it? You know, vouch for you, let her know that you've been nothing but professional on this project?"

"I don't know . . . do you think it would seem pre-meditated?"

"Not at all. I've learned with Gwen that you just have to deal with facts. I could simply tell her that nothing's happened between you and Devin, so why should she worry about it now?"

"Yeah, that still doesn't help with the fact that I withheld this information from her in the first place." I slouched in my chair.

"As hard-nosed as she comes across, I think Gwen knows deep down that you wouldn't cross her and understands that we all make mistakes." He looked at me through lowered eyebrows. "Speaking of which, I'd like to talk about last night."

I nodded slowly, not quite sure if I was ready for this. "Go on."

"What I said did not come out how I wanted it to, and when I tried to talk to you about it, it just got worse."

"Well, let's just put it out there. Why can't you work at Burton Relations anymore?" I held my breath, anticipating his answer.

"It's because of you."

My mind flooded with anger, hurt, fear, sadness, confusion, and a dozen other emotions I couldn't identify, or put into words.

Michael's face reddened, which I had never seen happen before. "No, no, no. That sounded bad. I didn't mean it, what I meant was—"

"I think I know what you meant." At this point I had stood up and was looking down at him. I hastily grabbed my purse but was eerily calm when I spoke. "I'm sorry if I've given you any reason for us to not work together. I've seen how smart you've been with this whole Devin thing, and I'm sad to be losing such a good coworker. I just wish that sometimes you'd think before you speak."

He grabbed my arm as I breezed past him. I ignored the rush I felt through my body. "You're right, I don't think before I speak, Kate, and unfortunately, it always seems to happen around you."

I pulled my arm away. "Well, I must be doing something to trigger this."

"You are. No, it's not what I meant! See, it's like I can't control it!" This was the most animated I had ever seen him.

"I don't believe this," I shook my head. "I feel more horrible than I did when Gwen nearly fired me this afternoon."

"That wasn't my intention. Please. You've gotta let me explain."

"Doesn't matter what the intention was." With that, I marched purposefully toward the door, ensuring that Billy's would never be voted "Most Charming Place to Grab a Cup of Coffee" in my book.

## Chapter Fifteen

About three blocks away from the coffee shop, my pace had slowed to normal. I didn't mind the idea of walking another ten blocks or so before getting a cab; it was the perfect antidote to the afternoon.

Had I been irrational in the coffee shop with Michael? I wish I could have blamed my behavior on PMS or a full moon, but neither of those was happening. Why did I let this man get under my skin? Should I have let Michael explain himself? But what was there to explain, really?

I replayed the scene at the coffee shop over and over in the cab I eventually caught, and I was so involved in it that I almost missed the limousine sedan parked outside my building.

The back door slowly opened, and there stood Devin. He wore a baby-blue polo shirt and khakis, like he was ready to hit the golf course, or pose for a cologne ad. He was the last person I wanted to see right now.

"Late night at the office?" he asked as I approached him.

"Nah, just got caught up with something."

"I was wondering if you'd be so kind as to join me for a drive." He smelled of whiskey.

I looked toward my apartment, then back at the limo. "You know, I really shouldn't," I said as I recalled my very recent conversation with Gwen. "It just wouldn't be good for business. Know what I mean?"

He shrugged. "It's not like I'm going to have my way with you . . . unless you want that, of course." He raised an eyebrow.

"Devin, please." I was in no mood for innuendo.

"What's going on?"

"It's really not worth mentioning."

"You look like you need to relax. Come on, let's go for a ride."

I stepped back. "Why are you even here?"

"I just wanted someone to talk to." He grinned slyly. "Okay, that's a lie. I wanted to talk to you."

I folded my arms. "I'm sure whatever you have to say to me can be said right here on this sidewalk."

Devin laughed and shook his head. "You're something else, Kate."

Here we go. "All right, what is it, Devin?" I reluctantly asked.

"I know I haven't been the easiest person to work with. I just thought that you deserved to hear how much I appreciate you."

"Did you have a life-changing experience?" I asked skeptically. His response was a coy shrug.

"So you stopped at my house and waited for me so you could tell me this?"

"Why not?"

I withdrew a deep breath, shaking my head. Devin grabbed my hand, but I immediately tugged it away. "Look, Dev, it's been a draining few months—no thanks to you, by the way—and I don't know what kind of mind game you're trying to play here. But if you just start behaving a little more I can be off this project, and we'll be out of each other's lives forever."

"Think about it," he intoned. "Have you seen anything but good things about me in the papers?"

I contemplated his point. Ever since Michael and I had started working with Devin, it felt like the vehicle was always in reverse. Almost every night we were at a benefit, a bar, a party, making sure that he was cast in the most favorable light possible and constantly steering him away from lecherous photographers—or Miranda Hamilton. I was so caught up in this world that I didn't even bother to realize that we might have actually been making progress.

This was it. This was what I was going to tell Gwen first thing Monday morning. Michael was right, Gwen only dealt in facts, not emotions, and if I had pulled together all the good press—and point out the lack of bad press—surrounding Devin, she might deem the project complete, exonerate me, promote me. No more Devin. But then again, no more Michael. I felt as if someone had just punched me in the stomach.

"What's going on in that head of yours?" Devin asked.

"Just putting all the pieces together, that's all."

With no warning, he leaned in and planted a sloppy, uninvited kiss on my lips. "You are so beautiful. Even more beautiful than you were the night of that benefit a few years back, in that picture of us."

I backed away from him and almost lost my balance. My jaw tightened. "Why would you bring up the night of the benefit?" Light bulb. "You jerk! You almost cost me my job! Why on earth would you have sent that picture to my boss?"

He tried to look sheepish. "Seemed like the thing to do. And for the record I am so attracted to you right now."

I glanced down at my wrinkled white blouse and black pants. I looked like a hostess at the Olive Garden, not to mention that I felt like I was trapped in a coffin, even though I had the cheerful sky above me and a soothing breeze blowing past.

"You need to leave. Now," I demanded.

"I'm sorry, I just got caught up in the moment."

"What moment? And even if there was a 'moment,' that's not a license to maul me."

"Isn't that what you wanted?"

"For crying out loud, Devin, you need to pull yourself together. I have not once in the last few months given you any indication that I wanted this to work out between us."

"Oh come on, maybe just a little fling?"

I looked into those blue eyes, wondering how they had such a power over me when we dated, and how they were repulsing me now. "I may not always have a grasp on what I want in life, but I know that you're not it."

I must have stung him. He immediately swung around toward his black limo sedan, got in the back seat, and slammed the door.

As I watched his car pull away, all I could think of was not Devin but Michael: how I should have given him a chance to speak his mind at the coffee shop. Maybe he did have a valid reason for not wanting to work together. Maybe I shouldn't have jumped to conclusions. Maybe I should've told him how I really felt about him.

I needed to call him, invite him over to talk. I ran up my stairs, but I froze once I got to my phone. Fear and anxiety lumped in my throat. How would I even address all this? How would I explain my erratic behavior? *"You could say sorry for starters,"* I said to myself.

I finally found the courage to pick up the phone, but not to dial his cell phone. I'd dial the first few numbers, then hit the power button on my phone.

For now, I had to focus on casting Devin out of our lives. After all, if Gwen realized how much progress we had made with Devin, she'd have to accept that the project was successful. And Fox himself complimented us on a job well done last night; shouldn't that speak volumes? I dragged my laptop out of its case and fervently started taking notes of the last two months. I couldn't help but smile, knowing that at least one loose end would soon be wrapped up.

But none of this stopped me from continually glancing at my phone. Maybe Michael would call, and I could explain my behavior, and he could explain his, and things would be all better. But as the hours went on, all was silent in my house. "Forget it," I grumbled and dialed Michael's cell. It rolled immediately to his voice mail.

"Hi, Michael, it's Kate." I hoped he wouldn't notice my trembling voice. "I'm sorry for running out of the coffee shop like that. I do want to talk, really. So, um, give me a call, and I hope to hear from you soon."

I tossed the cordless on the couch and watched it bounce off right onto the floor. I went back to taking notes on the computer and doing some online research, but in the back of my head, all I wanted was that phone to ring, and that it would be Michael on the other end.

## Chapter Sixteen

It had been a long time since I looked this forward to a Monday. Today I was going to have a clean slate. I was going to show Gwen all the newspaper articles, the columnists, the thank-you notes from charity event organizers, all boasting of how Devin was now a good guy, or at least as such in the eyes of the media. I had worked all weekend gathering up the evidence.

Granted, Gwen and Fox Underhill hadn't placed a timeline on the transformation (unless the words "do it soon" could be construed as a timeline), and they might still want us to have more substantial proof, but just like everything else in my job, I'd put a spin on it. "Tell me one item in a paper or magazine that has reflected poorly on Devin," I would say. And they couldn't, either. "Look at the praise he got from Partnership for the Homeless. You can't tell me this isn't progress?" Of course, in this grand scheme, Gwen would smile knowingly and approvingly, forgetting how I had wronged her just the Friday before.

Most of all, though, I couldn't wait to share the plan with Michael. He hadn't called me back all weekend, and yes, I had come up with a hundred excuses for why he never returned my call. ("Maybe he lost his phone" and "He hates me and never wants to speak with me again" were the two competing favorites.) But as much trepidation as I felt to see him, I had to do it.

I stepped into the office at 8:30. I unloaded my brief-case on my desk, hung up my tan belted trench coat, and peaked around the corner into Michael's office. The lights and computer were both off, and his chair was tucked neatly under his desk. It was uncharacteristic for him to arrive later than 7:30. Maybe he had an early-morning meeting, but the urge to talk to him at this moment overwhelmed me.

I walked around the office in search of an answer. "Good morning, Rita." I tried to sound nonchalant as I brushed past the front desk. "You haven't heard where Michael might be?"

"Got a voice mail late last night from him saying he would be out a few days due to a family emergency."

My face fell. "Is he okay? Did he say what happened?"

"Just a family emergency. That's all he said." Rita enunciated to me like a child who didn't quite understand an answer to a question. "Why don't you try his cell phone?"

"Nah, if it's a family emergency, I won't bother him. Thank you for your help." Rita shrugged, not nearly as concerned as I was with Michael's whereabouts.

On my way back to my office, I saw that Gwen's door was closed as she faced the window while talking on the phone. She only closed her door for serious conversations; she usually enjoyed making everyone else in the office uncomfortable with her loud voice and off-the-cuff remarks to clients. Maybe she was talking to someone about me, trying to find out if any of her counterparts would take on a lying, back-stabbing sycophant as a charity case. I really needed to talk to Michael so we could get things straightened out with each other, and then with Gwen.

I went back to my office. What were the odds that this was really a family emergency? I wondered as I held the phone receiver in one hand and pushed down the dial-tone button with the other. Would he have said something that drastic just to avoid talking to me? I've had plenty of "family emergencies" in my day—shopping, fatigue, or just not feeling like going into work. Then again, if it really was a family emergency, would I want to interrupt Michael with something as minute as this? On the other hand, he might not even have his cell on, and I could just leave him a message, in addition to the other one I left him on Friday night.

I was about to dial when Gwen stormed into my office; she scared the receiver right out of my hand.

"You are a genius! An absolute genius!" She mindlessly waved a newspaper through the air.

"Huh?"

"I knew you and Michael were doing good stuff on this project, but *this* blows me away!"

"What are you talking about?"

"You haven't seen today's *Post*?"

"Um, no, I've been a bit, uh, preoccupied."

"You don't look at the papers every morning?"

"Yeah, uh, sure, of course I do." Why was I lying again? Ugh. "You know what, Gwen? I don't look at the papers every morning, unless it's to do the crossword."

Gwen barked out a laugh. "You're too much. Trying to fool me into thinking you do the crossword."

So this is what telling the truth gets me? I needed to see what was in that newspaper, what was causing Gwen's sudden state of euphoria. She dropped the paper on my desk and plopped herself into the guest chair and watched me while I read it.

There, on Page Six, was a prominent shot of Devin whispering in Miranda Hamilton's ear. It must have been taken the first night they met. The headline blazed, *"Taming the Devil in Devin?"*

I looked up at Gwen, who was nodding vigorously, encouraging me to continue reading.

*Confirmed Manhattan bachelor Devin Underhill appears to have met his romantic match in America's sweetheart, Miranda Hamilton. The two have been seeing each other since Hamilton arrived in New York three months ago to shoot her new movie, "Talk Is Cheap." With a reputation as one of Hollywood's most generous—and genuine— starlets, Hamilton seems like an odd fit for Debonair Devin, but with his recent charity work, no doubt she was drawn to him, says a source close to the couple.*

*"That's probably what attracted Miranda to Devin, the fact that they both so strongly believe in the power of charitable giving," the source says. "Devin's really turned himself around and has become a better person, especially now that she's in his life."*

*Witnesses knew how serious Underhill was when they spotted him last week purchasing an engagement ring at Tiffany, running upwards of $300,000, according to the source.*

*While no one knows for sure when and how he officially proposed, the source confirms that they are both in Bermuda this week. "Don't be surprised if you hear about a mid-week wedding," the source says.*

I looked at Gwen disbelievingly.

"So, who was the 'source'—you or Michael?" she gawped.

"Well, I certainly can't take credit for it." Why would Michael do something like this and not tell me about it? Worse yet, how could all of this be happening right before my eyes, and I missed all the signs? "You didn't happen to hear from Michael today?"

"I heard about his family emergency. Maybe he's on his way to Bermuda to be the best man!" How apropos that Gwen thought this was the funniest thing she had ever heard. "Fox, of course, is thrilled," she continued. "I was just on the phone with him, and as far as he's concerned, we have done our jobs. Granted, he wishes his son would have told him of his plans, but who can complain when you're marrying someone like Miranda Hamilton? I'm telling you, her walking into our office was the best thing that ever happened to us."

"Speak for yourself," I mumbled inaudibly.

"What was that, my dear? You're not upset about this wedding, are you?"

"No, no. I'm, uh, I'm surprised that it got to the *Post* this fast, that's all."

She propped her middle-aged derriere on the corner of my desk. "Kate, you know how difficult it is for me to apologize, but I am sorry how I reacted on Friday. Had I known what you were up to, you little devil, I wouldn't have said anything! I was just keeping you on your toes, that's all."

"Well, it worked."

"Don't look like you're at a funeral, Brown!" Gwen leapt from my desk. "This is the best day ever in Burton Relations. I get to retire, you and Michael are going to be partners. There is one thing I think you should do, however."

"What's that?"

"Fly to Bermuda."

"Excuse me?" It was more of a harsh statement than a question.

"It'll be on me. Just take a little trip, say hi to the newlyweds, and come back in a few days. I'm assuming since you and Michael were such great matchmakers, they'd want you down there with them."

"I'm not so sure about that, Gwen. They've been

pretty private about this whole engagement." Private *and* shocking.

"You're going to have to do some follow-up press for them after they're married anyway, so don't consider this a request, consider this an order."

"What if I don't go?"

"I'd say you're an idiot for not going to a tropical paradise for free."

"Can't I just let Michael handle this one?"

"He's MIA, remember? Quit being such a ninny and just go," Gwen demanded.

I rose from my chair to become face to face with Gwen. "Fine," I succumbed. My mind was so clouded that I couldn't have put up a fight even if I'd wanted to. "I need to go home and pack. If you don't mind, I'll just finish up a few things around here."

"I'll have Rita book you a flight and a room at Hotel Bella, obviously." She left my office and shouted halfway across the hall. "Rita, get Kate on a flight to Bermuda immediately!"

I re-read the article. *"That's probably what attracted Miranda to Devin, the fact that they both so strongly believe in the power of charitable giving."* Devin could care less about charities before we got our hands on him. *Witnesses knew how serious Underhill was when they spotted him last week purchasing an engagement ring at Tiffany.*

How did I not know this? All along Michael insisted that Miranda was not interested in Devin, and she her-self made that pretty clear too. Had Devin finally won her over behind the scenes? And if he really was engaged, he had no business trying to kiss me on Friday. Something wasn't adding up.

I had grown to consider Miranda a—gulp—friend, and because of that, I felt this sense of obligation to warn her about the fact that her fiancé was hitting on an ex-girlfriend days before their wedding. For that reason alone, I could justify going to Bermuda.

Where was Michael? I needed to know what, if any, role he played in this mess. Perhaps "family emergency" meant staying out of the office until the fallout had cleared. I had to call him, but I needed to make another call to someone who might help put some of the pieces of this obtuse puzzle together.

"Hello," a groggy voice answered.

"Anna, it's me. Why aren't you at work?"

"They didn't need me until later in the week since we're shooting extras only. No Miranda for a few days."

"Yeah, about that. Do you know where she went?"

"Bermuda, I think. Why?"

"I'd tell you to grab a *New York Post*, but since you just woke up, I'll give you the abridged version. Did you know that she and Devin are eloping?"

"What!" I knew that would jolt Anna into the waking world.

"You didn't happen to see Devin hanging around the set, did you?"

She paused thoughtfully. "Not that I can remember, Kate. But they keep us makeup people pretty sheltered, so I'm not the best person to ask. I can find out for you, though."

"It doesn't matter at this point, but thanks anyway."

"How did this slip past you?"

"That's the question I can't stop asking myself. I mean, we're with this guy what feels like day and night for the last three months, and to hear something like this . . . it's unbelievable. Of course, Gwen thinks I just cured cancer. You know what the worst part is?"

"Can you even pick a worst part?" Anna was fully awake and engaged in the conversation.

"Devin was waiting for me Friday night at my house. We're standing outside, when he decides to tell me how wonderful I am and kisses me."

"What in the world?" Anna fumed.

"I know!"

"You slapped him across the face, right?"

"Even better. I told him that I didn't want him."

Anna squealed. "Girl, you're right, that *is* better than a boring old slap!" She paused. "You know, it just doesn't sound like Miranda. Why would she do this knowing that she's returning to California in a month?"

"Love makes us do crazy things, or so I'm told."

"Are you sure it's even true? After all, it seems awfully suspicious that you wouldn't know. What's Michael's take on all of this?"

"Don't know. He had a family emergency today."

"How convenient."

"I'm trying to give him the benefit of the doubt, but I'm sure he doesn't want to hear from me after I stormed out of the coffee shop on him on Friday."

"Why didn't you call me this weekend and tell me any of this?" Anna sounded offended.

"I'm sorry, hon, but I was so wrapped up in formulating how to tell Michael that I'm feeling something for him, and in proving my worth to Gwen after she almost fired me last week that I—"

"Let me get this straight. You almost got fired, you're finally admitting your feelings for Michael, and you told your ex to buzz off? And you forgot to call your best friend?"

Guilt washed over me. "I'm sorry. I've been so caught up in my own world that I haven't been letting anyone in." Including Michael, I now realized.

"You know I'm just teasing you. Phone works both ways, they say. I'm just glad that we're talking now." Anna hesitated. "There's something I've been meaning to ask you about too."

"Shoot."

"So, Miranda has—"

Rita appeared in my door. "Anna, can you hold on a sec?"

She tossed paperwork onto my desk. "You leave in three hours."

"Wow, that's efficient. Thanks, Rita." I put my mouth back up to the phone. "Crap. I'm sorry, Anna, but I need to run home before catching my flight to Bermuda. Can I call you from the airport?"

"You're going to Bermuda?"

"Woops, guess I left out another minor detail. It's not for fun. Gwen has kind of pushed me into going to do some spin control for something I didn't even know about in the first place. Lord knows I shouldn't go as a matter of principle, but apparently I'm in self-torture mode. If nothing else, I have to get Miranda out of this jam."

"Good luck. If you don't have time to call me from the airport, don't worry. We'll catch up soon enough. Be safe, now go! You've got a very important flight waiting for you."

## Chapter Seventeen

"I'm wondering if you could tell me if Devin Underhill is staying in his penthouse," I asked the Hotel Bella concierge as sweetly as I could.

"Ma'am, you know we don't give out that kind of information," he kindly but firmly answered.

"But I'm his publicist."

"If that's the case, you should know where he is," he smirked.

"What if I told you he was in grave danger?" I almost laughed at myself for trying to be so mysterious.

"Then I'm sure we'll take care of it." The concierge walked to a back room, likely calling security to drag the crazy lady away.

I slumped on one of the plush gold chairs in the open-air lobby. Despite my reasons for being here, I couldn't help but smile at the warm, lilac-scented breeze that blew over me. And the locals (except the concierge, unfortunately) were so helpful, so welcoming. Someone on this island had to be able to help me; Devin was a familiar face here. He came to Bermuda at least once a month, always telling me when we dated that this island was his home away from home.

For now, I had to keep watch. I was afraid to bring my luggage up to my room, because Murphy's Law indicates that the minute I left my post, Devin would appear. So I crossed my legs and stared at the front entrance. I really needed a hobby, as I was being left alone too often with my thoughts.

I robotically bit my nails, contemplating whether I should get on the next plane home. Despite the green, lush beauty of the island, I had no business being here. What if Miranda and Devin really were happy together? Then I would just be the jerk who tried to break them up, and who knows what would happen with my career then? As far as Michael goes, I tried him on his cell one last time while I rushed to get my seat on the plane, but his phone was still turned off. I didn't leave him a message.

I saw a tall, tanned man get out of a taxi and walk toward the entrance of the hotel. Heart thumping, I rose from my seat thinking the man was Devin, but as he came closer, I realized it was just a stranger. I sat back down, but knew that I couldn't wait here by myself much longer. This island wasn't that big; if I didn't see him at the hotel, I was bound to run into him somewhere else. So I rolled my luggage behind me and dropped it off in my room on the king-sized bed.

I went behind the property, which was located right

on the ocean. The pristine, pink-tinged sand was almost surreal. The salt of the crystal-clear sea hung in the hot, humid air. My only regret was that I didn't change clothes before I left the hotel room. I was still wearing a blue v-neck sweater and jeans from the flight, and I already could feel the shirt sticking to my back.

I scoured the beach for any sign of Miranda and Devin. From a distance, I saw a couple lounging on a blanket, feeding each other fruit and giggling. I knew it wasn't Miranda and Devin, but watching that happy pair, oddly enough, made me really miss Michael.

There was a lot of activity further up the beach. The closer I got, I noticed people frantically running around, with lots of headsets and cell phones. Upon even closer review, I saw a bunch of tall lights and a large white canopy. This was it. This was the site of the wedding.

I looked around for a familiar face, but I didn't see anyone. I consciously sighed. Maybe this was someone else's party. And that's when I saw Miranda.

She stood in a white bikini, showing off her incredibly-shaped abs and tanned body. She looked serious while a man in a white T-shirt holding a clipboard asked her questions and took notes. When he moved to the side, Michael was in clear view. He walked over to Miranda and put an arm around her shoulder.

This is why Michael couldn't work with me; he was in love with Miranda and was probably moving back to California with her. Ohhh, what am I doing here? I thought desperately. I had never felt so humiliated, so ashamed, so depressed in my life. I backed away before they could see me, but I tripped over one of the electric chords and landed ever-so-ungracefully in the sand, right on my bottom.

"Kate!" Miranda bounded over to me, looking a lot like Bo Derek in *10*, sans the gold bathing suit and braids. "I can't believe you're here."

Michael was right behind her, looking happy yet extremely confused.

"I can't believe I'm here, either," I mumbled. I tried to nonchalantly look for a huge diamond sparkler on Miranda's left ring finger, but it was empty.

"What are you doing here?" At this point Michael had extended his hand to pull me out of the sand.

"There's, well, I can't . . ." Deep breath, gather thoughts. "Don't marry Devin!" I blurted. "Or Michael!" And I had accused Michael of not thinking before he spoke?

Miranda looked at Michael with daggers practically coming out of her eyes. "You didn't tell her?" This was the least amiable I had ever seen her. Michael hung his head, then looked away.

"I don't believe this." Miranda put her hands on her hips. "My big *brother* here didn't tell you that we're related."

I thought I was going to end up in the sand again. "S-s-siblings?" I stuttered.

Michael stepped toward me. "Kate, I know that I've said this a lot in the last few days, but let me explain."

"Why didn't you tell me?" My face fell.

"To his credit," Miranda jumped in, "we've had an agreement that we would not let anyone know we were brother and sister. He didn't want to be an actor, and I already was getting some parts on TV. He wanted to get his foot in the door in PR without the help of his famous sister." She shook her head sympathetically. "I thought for sure he would tell you, considering how he feels about you."

"Feels about me?" I meekly parroted.

"You're making it worse," Michael hissed at his sister.

Miranda threw her hands up in the air. "Well, from what I'm seeing and hearing, you're not doing a very good job at telling her yourself."

"I really do have a good excuse for why I haven't called you back," Michael said sheepishly as he stepped even closer to me.

"I'm all ears." I clasped my shaking hands together.

"Miranda called me last night saying that her agent warned her about this false report that was going to appear in the *Post* today."

"Little did I know I was marrying Devin Underhill this week," she added dryly. "So, Michael came down to give me moral support in case I ran into Devin."

I looked between the two of them expectantly. "So, what happened?"

"Devin showed up on the set a few times in the last month or so," Miranda said.

"Uninvited," Michael interjected.

"I blew him off, but I didn't want to make a big scene, since I know what you guys were trying to do and that he needed good press."

My brow was furrowed. "How did he make the leap from that to an engagement?"

Michael crossed his arms. "Apparently he knew about Miranda's trip to Bermuda and was overconfident that she would say yes. So he leaked the story to the *Post*."

"You just missed him, Kate." Miranda smiled ironically. "He was about to get down on one knee, but I stopped him. I told him I wasn't interested in him romantically."

I threw my hand over my mouth. "How did he react to that?"

"Kind of shocked, actually." Miranda shook her head.

"And don't forget the stomping off in a huff," Michael helpfully added. "I got to witness the whole thing."

"And what was his reaction to you, Michael?"

"Very confused. Couldn't figure out why I was here. Then he looked like he wanted to punch me, but instead, he stomped off."

"Thank God I have people like you and Michael in my life." Miranda spoke kindly. "I just feel like I contributed to this problem somehow."

I put my hand on her arm. "Don't worry about it. You have nothing to do with this." I turned to Michael. "What do we do about Devin now? I mean, Gwen thinks we're the ones responsible for this, and if she finds out that we let this hoax slip past us . . ."

Michael grabbed my hand. "After the stunt he pulled today, I don't think we'll be hearing from Devin in a really long time."

The man with the clipboard walked up to Miranda. "Ms. Hamilton, we're ready to start the photo shoot."

She put her arms around both our shoulders. "Well,

kids, they need me. And it's a good thing, too, because you two have some catching up to do." She pointed at Michael. "And remember what I told you." She swayed toward the set.

I tilted my head. "What did she tell you?"

He looked down at me with a smile forming at his lips. "Not to be a dumb boy and screw it up this time."

Lovely, lovely Miranda. I'd definitely have to thank her for her words of wisdom later.

"You have a captive audience," I grinned, but suddenly became very serious. "So let's start with why we can't work together anymore."

"Remember when I told you about my ex-fiancée, that after her I vowed never to get involved with a coworker again?" I nodded encouragingly. "I knew that I was, er, starting to feel something for you, and I didn't want to ruin a good thing between us, so in my head, I thought it was best if I left Burton Relations in the hopes that something could work out between us. But of course, when I tried to tell you that, I sounded like a complete goon."

"I didn't help the cause much, running out on you at both the benefit and the coffee shop. Did you get my voice mail?" I asked hopefully.

"Not if you left it on my cell phone. I sort of, well, dropped it."

I pursed my lips, and Michael continued. "When you left the coffee shop, I was so mad at myself. I fumbled around for my cell phone to call you, but I was so jittery it slipped out of my hand and fell right into my coffee. Needless to say, I haven't had time to look for a new one." He gave an embarrassed grin.

"Why didn't you tell me about Miranda being your sister?"

"I tried that night we had Chinese at your place, but then we were interrupted, and I just didn't want to talk to you about it."

I must've looked hurt, because Michael gave me a comforting rub on my shoulder. "See, there I go again, my mouth running faster than I can keep up with. I just didn't want it to be a burden to you, so I didn't bring it up, but I kept thinking about it." He shook his head in spite of himself. "Miranda says I live in my head too much."

I belted out a hearty laugh. "That's what Anna says about me! We're quite the pair."

And suddenly, Michael grabbed my hands, which were shaking. "I think we *are* quite the pair. I just need to know you feel the same way. And that you'll forgive me for saying anything that made you feel less special than you are."

I wanted to collapse into his arms and be held. But for now, just being here with Michael in paradise was enough for me.

And, with all the courage I could muster, I told him what was brewing within me. "Of course I have feelings for you, Michael. How else can you explain my running out on you twice in twenty-four hours? I just need to ask one thing. Please don't leave Burton Relations."

He drew me into a tight embrace, his strong arms engulfing me. "Not without you," he tenderly whispered into my hair. Michael backed away from me and stared into my eyes before closing his hazel eyes and placing his warm, soft lips on mine. And I can honestly say that it was the most unexpected, most wonderful kiss a man has ever given me.

We broke away from each other's mouths and giggled. We saw Miranda sashaying toward us with a wide, giddy grin. She handed me her cell phone. "It's Anna. I'm sorry, but I had to call and tell her about the two of you! Don't be mad!" She handed the phone to me, then skipped back to the set.

"Glad to see you both got smart," Anna said smugly.

"And all it took was getting out of the country. Look, I'm sorry I was so rushed this morning when we talked. You were going to tell me something, and we got interrupted. What's going on?"

Anna cleared her throat. "Miranda has invited me to be her personal make-up artist. In Hollywood."

"What? That's fantastic! I am so excited for you, Anna." I gleamed, but my heart hurt at the same time. My best friend, the one who's been there with me for the last ten years, was going away. But how could I be upset at the opportunity of a lifetime for her?

I heard Anna sniffle. "I mean, you'll be coming out to visit me, right?"

"Every chance I get. When are you leaving?"

"Well, I've found someone to sublet my place for now. Miranda has found me a great place in Santa Monica, so sometime within the next month, I'd say."

"I'm going to miss you so much." I started to tear up.

Anna was crying, too. "Now, this is a happy time, remember? And from what I hear, you're in very good hands." I looked over at Michael, whose eyes had been on me the whole time.

"Okay, I'll be back in a few days," I said with mixed emotions. "We'll have a big going-away party and I'll be at your place every day helping with packing and just hanging out with you." I sighed. "You're gonna be great in Hollywood. I just know it."

"Thanks for being so supportive. Anyway, I better run. Call me when you get back. And be careful with Michael!" She joked. "I hear he's fragile."

"Take care, hon."

I wiped a renegade tear off my cheekbone. Michael walked over to me and wrapped his arms around my waist. "So, she's going to L.A., huh?"

I nodded lightly, then rested my head on his shoulder. He tipped my head up so he could look me directly in the eye. "I think that we should do dinner and stare dreamily into each other's eyes." Michael winked.

I playfully slapped his wrist. "And maybe crack each other up with more Ralphie Wiggum lines?"

He hugged me tightly again. "I wouldn't have it any other way."

We walked toward the photo shoot, where Miranda was posing in the evening sun.

"You two be good!" She shouted from the set. "I'll call you tomorrow."

"I, um, I'm staying at Hotel Bella, unfortunately," I muttered to Michael.

"We're getting you out of that hotel," he grinned coyly.

I gave him my forearm. "Twist, twist!" He took my

arm, fervently pulled me in, and kissed me with a passion that I'll never forget. This, I thought as he gently worked his fingers through my hair, was something I could finally put a positive spin on.

## Epilogue

So I was wrong about a few things. First, I found out why Gwen was so eager to take on the Devin project. It was not her desire to be with Fox—rather, her desire to be with his property. At the start of the arrangement, Fox said that if Gwen and her team had helped get Devin in line, she could stay in one of his Portuguese villas for six months. She took that as her signal for early retirement, and made good on her word. Within two months of our trip to Bermuda, Michael and I became partners in Burton Relations.

Second, I was convinced that the Devin makeover would backfire once Miranda rejected him. Instead, he entirely disappeared from the social scene. No more parties, no more coverage in the tabloids. Fortunately, Fox never knew it was Devin who announced his fake engagement to the *Post*. He was, however, thrilled that

Devin had so much time to devote to Hotel Bella now that he was flying under the social radar.

But I was right on a few things. I knew that Anna would thrive in Hollywood. In fact, within three months of her being out there, she was already booked as lead makeup artist on six major movies. And I was right when I said I would miss her terribly. And she was right that I had a nice distraction.

About that distraction. Michael and I have been dating for three months now, and every day it gets better. Our business partnership works well too. We've already gotten four new clients. We do make it a point to keep the personal separate from the professional. And things have been *very* personal.

Everything about Michael and our relationship just feels right. Not very New York or ironic of me, but I'll take it.